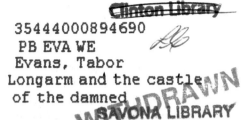

Lon

Longar...
it. Both...

The one to the left of the doorway pointed something under his duster—a sawed-off shotgun as it turned out—but had no time to fire before Longarm's bullet smashed into his breastbone, taking first the breath away from him and then his life as he was launched backward against the stone building blocks.

The man on the right, much closer to Longarm, tried to swivel around before the lawman could fire a second shot.

He was late and he damn well knew it . . . He turned ghost pale and bolted for the wide open spaces.

Longarm thought about putting a bullet in the bastard's back but there seemed no point to that. He aimed a foot or so over the man's head and triggered a .45 slug. He would not have thought it possible, but the fellow managed to run even faster after that sizzler pinked the crown of his hat, sending the hat and the man flying.

City police and sheriff's deputies came boiling out of the courthouse in response to the sudden gunfire, but Longarm's two shots ended the conflict.

"What the hell . . . ?"

Longarm shrugged and reloaded his revolver. "I think somebody didn't want me to testify this mornin' . . ."

DON'T MISS THESE
ALL-ACTION WESTERN SERIES
FROM THE BERKLEY PUBLISHING GROUP

THE GUNSMITH by J. R. Roberts
  Clint Adams was a legend among lawmen, outlaws, and ladies. They called him . . . the Gunsmith.

LONGARM by Tabor Evans
  The popular long-running series about Deputy U.S. Marshal Custis Long—his life, his loves, his fight for justice.

SLOCUM by Jake Logan
  Today's longest-running action Western. John Slocum rides a deadly trail of hot blood and cold steel.

BUSHWHACKERS by B. J. Lanagan
  An action-packed series by the creators of Longarm! The rousing adventures of the most brutal gang of cutthroats ever assembled—Quantrill's Raiders.

DIAMONDBACK by Guy Brewer
  Dex Yancey is Diamondback, a Southern gentleman turned con man when his brother cheats him out of the family fortune. Ladies love him. Gamblers hate him. But nobody pulls one over on Dex . . .

WILDGUN by Jack Hanson
  The blazing adventures of mountain man Will Barlow—from the creators of Longarm!

TEXAS TRACKER by Tom Calhoun
  J.T. Law: the most relentless—and dangerous—manhunter in all Texas. Where sheriffs and posses fail, he's the best man to bring in the most vicious outlaws—for a price.

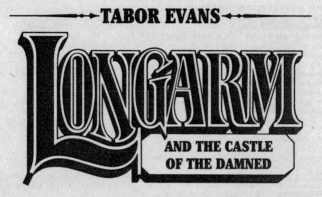

‹·‹ TABOR EVANS ›·›

LONGARM

AND THE CASTLE OF THE DAMNED

JOVE BOOKS, NEW YORK

THE BERKLEY PUBLISHING GROUP
Published by the Penguin Group
Penguin Group (USA) Inc.
375 Hudson Street, New York, New York 10014, USA
Penguin Group (Canada), 90 Eglinton Avenue East, Suite 700, Toronto, Ontario M4P 2Y3, Canada
(a division of Pearson Penguin Canada Inc.)
Penguin Books Ltd., 80 Strand, London WC2R 0RL, England
Penguin Group Ireland, 25 St. Stephen's Green, Dublin 2, Ireland (a division of Penguin Books Ltd.)
Penguin Group (Australia), 250 Camberwell Road, Camberwell, Victoria 3124, Australia
(a division of Pearson Australia Group Pty. Ltd.)
Penguin Books India Pvt. Ltd., 11 Community Centre, Panchsheel Park, New Delhi—110 017, India
Penguin Group (NZ), 67 Apollo Drive, Rosedale, Auckland 0632, New Zealand
(a division of Pearson New Zealand Ltd.)
Penguin Books (South Africa) (Pty.) Ltd., 24 Sturdee Avenue, Rosebank, Johannesburg 2196,
South Africa

Penguin Books Ltd., Registered Offices: 80 Strand, London WC2R 0RL, England

This is a work of fiction. Names, characters, places, and incidents either are the product of the author's imagination or are used fictitiously, and any resemblance to actual persons, living or dead, business establishments, events, or locales is entirely coincidental.

LONGARM AND THE CASTLE OF THE DAMNED

A Jove Book / published by arrangement with the author

PRINTING HISTORY
Jove edition / November 2011

Copyright © 2011 by Penguin Group (USA) Inc.
Cover illustration by Milo Sinovcic.

ISBN: 978-0-515-15010-0

JOVE®
Jove Books are published by The Berkley Publishing Group,
a division of Penguin Group (USA) Inc.,
375 Hudson Street, New York, New York 10014.
JOVE® is a registered trademark of Penguin Group (USA) Inc.
The "J" design is a trademark of Penguin Group (USA) Inc.

PRINTED IN THE UNITED STATES OF AMERICA

10 9 8 7 6 5 4 3 2 1

Chapter 1

There is nothing else as boring as a damned murder trial, Deputy United States Marshal Custis Long silently grumbled as he sat on the hard courtroom bench waiting to be called as a witness. Long, called Longarm by friends and enemies alike, stifled a yawn behind his fist and concentrated on what had been the focus of his attention for much of the past three days.

While the opposing lawyers worried about dotting every "i" and crossing every "t," Longarm sat there watching a most intriguing young woman who for two of those days had been seated on the defense's side of the stuffy room, situated squarely in front of Longarm. He could not have missed seeing her had he tried.

He guessed her to be in her early to mid twenties, with light brown hair, a slender build, and a face that belonged on an angel. Her dress—she had worn the same one both days—had gone out of style decades earlier, yet the girl had a presence, the way she carried herself or simply because of her natural beauty, that made the rather shabby, dark green garment seem the height of fashion.

It might have been just his imagination, but Longarm would almost have sworn that today she was looking back at him while he watched her.

Not that he considered himself all that worthy of admiration. He was three inches over six feet in height, lean, with wide shoulders and a horseman's narrow waist. His hair and mustache were a dark seal brown, and his face was craggy and leather-tanned from years of exposure to the elements.

He was far from being handsome, yet there was something about him that made women tend to melt when he approached them. He did not really understand this—there was nothing in a mirror that he could find all that interesting—but he certainly did not complain about it.

Today, as on most days, he wore a light brown tweed coat, a flat-crowned brown Stetson, brown corduroy trousers, black gunbelt rigged for a cross-draw, and black, calf-high cavalry boots.

Having ridden out of Chief U.S. Marshal William Vail's Denver office, Longarm currently was in Cheyenne, Wyoming Territory, waiting to testify in the murder trial of one James Henry Willoughby, despite murder being a state or territorial crime and not a federal offense.

Six months earlier Longarm had sought Willoughby on a federal warrant for interference with the delivery of the mail. A young constable with the Evanston police force offered to guide Longarm to the shack where Willoughby was said to be holed up.

The man was there, all right. As soon as he saw Constable Harvey Franks, Willoughby opened fire, killing Franks with a blast from a shotgun.

Longarm fired back, and if the son of a bitch had done the decent thing and died there and then, the deputy marshal would have been spared the discomfort of sitting through this interminable trial now. Instead Willoughby was wounded, gave himself up, and had been behind bars ever since.

Hopefully he would hang shortly after the trial concluded, but first the lawyers had to earn their fees. It was already clear that the defense was setting something up, but Longarm did not see what the hell it would be. After all, he'd stood right there and watched when Willoughby gunned the constable down in cold blood.

That would be a hard nut for the defense to crack when it finally came time for Longarm to testify. He was being held back for the last of the prosecution's case. The lead prosecutor had told him as much. He understood the trial strategy, but he would have liked it better if he could just have said his piece and then been on his way to more interesting things.

Like that pretty woman over there.

He had in his imagination undressed her so many times over the past two days that all he had to do now was glimpse the back of her neck and he could get a hard-on.

She was prim and proper and very likely still a virgin, but that did not stop him from thinking about what she would look like without all that cloth enveloping her figure. She very likely . . .

A rap of Judge Thornton's gavel brought Longarm's attention back from the realm of reverie and into dull reality.

He straightened his shoulders and tried to look awake.

"We will be in recess until ten o'clock tomorrow morning," Thornton declared with another loud bang of the gavel.

The lawyers at both tables began clearing away their papers and volumes of law books, while no fewer than four local constables and two sheriff's deputies took charge of the prisoner, hustling the man quickly out of the courtroom before any of his rather large crowd of sympathizers could speak to him.

Longarm stood, stretched, and yawned hugely. He intended to have a glass—or two—of good rye whiskey and then perhaps a steak at Houlihan's Chop House. Why not? He was on an expense account during the trial, the Evanston Police Department providing for his needs until his testimony had been presented. Let the city pay for a good meal then.

He glanced across the room and noticed that the lady with the light brown hair already disappeared. He rather hoped she would be back tomorrow, as she was much nicer to look at than the jurors, most of whom appeared to be half-asleep while the lawyers droned on. And on. And on.

Now the jury was being escorted out by the court bailiff, lest they be contaminated by comments from the spectators.

Longarm yawned again and started for the door.

As soon as he stepped through it, he was confronted by the lady in the bottle green dress.

"Excuse me, sir, but you appear to be a gentleman. Would you think me too bold if I asked you to escort me to dinner. I . . . I can pay. For you too, I mean. But I couldn't possibly go alone into a public establishment like that. Is . . . Would that be all right, sir?"

Gentleman? It was not just every day that Custis Long was called that. He gave the lady a half bow and offered his arm.

What else could he possibly do?

Chapter 2

"Excuse me, sir. Could I have your attention for a moment, sir?"

The elderly, very wrinkled, and timeworn fellow was holding a broom. Longarm thought he recalled seeing the man around the courthouse a time or two before now. A beggar, Longarm immediately thought. An old man trying to cadge a quarter for a shot and a beer and a bowl of chili.

Normally Longarm would have had a moment to spare as well as a dime or so, but not this evening, not while the pretty young thing was already on his arm.

"Later," he growled, regretting at once the rough tone. It was not the old boy's fault. Still, words once spoken cannot be recalled. "Sorry," he amended over his shoulder as he guided the young woman out the front doors of the handsome courthouse. "See me later."

She looked up at him—lordy, she had the prettiest blue eyes and the longest eyelashes—as if to question him.

"Just a beggar," Longarm told her. "I'll give him something tomorrow."

The girl smiled—damn, she did have a nice smile; dimples too—and said, "You are a very nice gentleman, sir."

Longarm was finding it increasingly difficult to walk beside this girl without the front of his britches preceding him by half a foot or more. The girl just plain had that effect on him.

"I intended to eat at Houlihan's tonight," he told her. "Would that be acceptable?"

"So long as it is not . . . rough," she said. "Strangers frighten me."

"It's a nice place," he said, "or so I hear tell."

She gave him that smile again. "In your company, I believe I should feel safe anywhere."

The evening, he thought, was looking up.

"My name is Lenore Bailey." Smile. "And of course I know who you are. Practically everyone does." Smile. "I must admit that I noticed you in the gallery and I . . . Well, the truth is that I inquired about you." Smile.

Oh, yes, Longarm thought. This evening was most definitely looking up.

They dined sumptuously on green salad—courtesy of the Union Pacific's fast freight from California—lamb chops, and new potatoes. And a bottle and a half of dago red, which the lady seemed not to know enough to tell that it was a raw and inferior wine. For not knowing anything about spirits, though, she drank enough of it. She seemed nervous and more than a little tiddly.

"Marshal Long," she asked when the meal was concluded and they were about to leave, "would you mind escorting me to my room now? I feel . . . I feel not so very steady on my feet."

"I would be honored, Miss Bailey." He offered his arm again.

"It is the Crenley house," she said. "I know the owner.

She happens to be visiting in Denver, but she gave me permission to stay there."

"I don't know it," he said.

She smiled. "I shall show you."

And she did. Not only to the house but inside. There were no furnishings in the parlor, so she said, "Follow me. We can sit back here."

The girl led the way toward the back of the house, where there was a kitchen and beyond it a small bedroom that held a narrow bed and an upended keg that served as a dressing table.

He thought about mentioning how sparsely furnished her friend's house was, but Lenore sat on the bed and patted a spot immediately beside her. "Please sit down. There is something I want to tell you." She sounded very serious when she said that, so Longarm dutifully sat.

The next thing he knew, Lenore's arms were around his neck and her tongue was in his mouth.

Oh, yes. This evening was most definitely looking up.

Chapter 3

Lenore shed her clothes as slick as skinning a rabbit and just as quickly started in on Longarm's duds. She opened the buttons of his fly while he was still getting his shirt undone, and when she saw what she found there, she moaned with pleasure.

"What a handsome gentleman," she said, but this time he was pretty sure it was not his face she referred to. His dick, standing tall and as hard as a rock, was throbbing only inches in front of the girl's face, and all of her attention seemed to be on it.

Lenore herself was slim and sleek and pretty. Her tits were soft and sagged more than a little once the foundation garments were removed. But he was able to forgive her for that.

She slipped the pins out of her hair and shook her head, shaking out a cascade of brown that framed her face.

He could feel her breath on the engorged head of his cock. Then she dipped her head forward. Her lips parted and her tongue played with the underside of his glans, while her fingers worked a sort of magic with his balls and the sensitive flat between his balls and his asshole.

"You smell nice," she muttered. "It's a man smell. I love it."

What he loved was what Lenore was doing to him.

Her lips parted a little further, and she mouthed the head of his cock, taking it slowly into the heat of her mouth then swishing it back and forth in there while her tongue continued to lave the head and, soon, the length of his shaft, as she took him deeper and deeper into her throat.

Longarm sagged back onto the bed, his eyes nearly closing as powerful sensations of pleasure overtook him.

Lenore cupped his balls in one palm while the fingers of her other hand steadied his cock and held it in place so she could better press herself onto him.

"So big," she mumbled once when she withdrew enough that his cock was poised at the opening of her lips.

Then she pushed her mouth back onto him, shoving herself forward until his prick filled her mouth and drove on through, past the ring of cartilage at the back of her throat and beyond.

The feelings she gave him were extraordinary.

She stayed with him until the sweet pressure built beyond containing and he exploded into her mouth, his jism squirting in a nearly continuous flow.

Lenore gobbled and gulped and at one point choked . . . but she stayed with him until he was done flowing. She swallowed everything he gave her and acted like she wanted even more.

"Nice" was all she said when she finally withdrew.

She sat up and smiled—ah, those dimples and lovely blue eyes—then quite happily arranged herself on the bed with her legs parted, ready for his entry.

Longarm obliged, first taking her left nipple into his

mouth and rolling it with his tongue. Lenore groaned and her hips began to lift and writhe.

He slipped a finger into her pussy and found she was dripping wet and more than ready for him. He moved overtop of her, and Lenore reached between them to grasp his cock and guide it inside her, as Longarm lowered herself onto her. Into her. Deep. Deeper. Filling her body with his cock.

He raised himself enough that he could see the rapt look on her face.

Then he began to pump into her, slowly at first and then quicker and quicker, until he was pounding her belly with his own.

Lenore's moans filled his right ear, and her hips rose and fell in a frantic rhythm, until she cried out, clutching at him with arms and legs alike. And clenching his pecker tight with her spasming pussy.

Longarm felt the rising of his sap, and for the second time in a space of only minutes he came, jets of hot cum squirting deep inside the girl's body.

When both were silent, sated, he looked into her eyes and said, "Remind me t'feed you right regular if that's the reaction it gets outa you."

Lenore laughed and nibbled on his earlobe.

"Careful, darlin'," he said, "lest you get me started again."

"In that case," she told him . . . and again began chewing on the earlobe.

Longarm woke slowly and stretched. He had just awakened from a full night's sleep but still felt drained.

He was, he discovered, entwined limb to limb with Lenore Bailey, she being the reason he felt so drained.

It was unusual for him to spend the night with a woman

he did not know, but Lenore was an exception. She was . . . well, she was no virgin, that was for damn sure. But there was something about her that seemed almost innocent.

He yawned and looked around. First at the way Lenore's eyelashes looked so sweet and childlike against her cheek, then at the nearly empty room where they'd spent the night. There was daylight showing around the edges of the blind drawn across the window at the back of the room.

He carefully disentangled himself from Lenore's embrace, sat up, and retrieved his vest from the bare floor. He pulled out his watch and key, inserted the key into the Ingersoll and carefully wound it—in the activities of the night he had forgotten to do that—then checked the time. He should have time for a cup of coffee at the café before court resumed for the day. He was fairly sure he would be called to testify today, so he did not want to be late.

"Darling Custis," Lenore whispered, reaching for him. "Kiss me."

He did, one hand almost on its own finding her breast and kneading the soft flesh there, the nipple suddenly hard beneath his palm.

"Take me, Custis. Do me." She found his limp cock and toyed with it, quickly bringing it back to raging readiness. She cupped his balls and gently pulled, urging him onto her. Into her.

Longarm considered the time. And smiled. He did not really have to have that cup of coffee.

He climbed into the saddle yet again, once more amazed that a girl could look so sweet and yet act so bawdy.

He stroked deep into her, deliberately pushing the rhythm so that the sensations quickly built then spilled over into a hard, hammering climax that might well leave the girl black and blue in her more tender parts.

His climax was so hard, so complete that he cried aloud

when the fluids gushed out of him and into her slender body. Lenore held him tight, wrapping her legs around him and holding on.

Longarm tried to pull away from her, but Lenore held on all the tighter.

"Now, looka here, darlin', I have to get to court this mornin'. I'm gonna have to testify today. I'm pretty sure about that."

"No, Custis, don't leave me. Please." She pulled away but only long enough to slip down onto the floor and put her pretty head in his lap, lifting his cock, still wet and sticky from inside her body, and sucking it into her mouth. She lifted her head long enough to mumble, "Stay with me, Custis. You must. Please."

"I can't do it, darlin'. Now, leave me be. I got to go."

He was pretty sure that now there was no time for that coffee. Not that he regretted the distraction. Far from it. Lenore Bailey was one sweet piece of ass. And she gave a mean blow job too.

"Let go, darlin'. I got to get dressed."

Lenore continued to suck on him. The damn girl was becoming annoying.

"Dammit, Lenore, I got to go now."

She quit stroking his balls and reached underneath the bed. When her hand appeared again, she was holding a four-shot Sharps derringer.

Lenore raised her head and said, "I can't let you do that, Custis. Don't argue with me now. We'll spend the day in bed, you and me. You won't regret it, I promise. We'll have us a fine old time fucking our brains out." She gave him a questioning look and said, "Please, Custis? Please?"

Longarm looked into the four barrels of the little Sharps. They were not very big.

But the damn gun was big enough.

"Stay with me, Custis. You have to."

She surely did seem to mean that too. As in *You have to or I'll put a bullet in your brisket.*

"Shit," he murmured. "You don't give a boy much of a choice, do you?"

Lenore smiled. "Thank you, Custis. You won't regret this. I promise." She reached for his cock again.

Chapter 4

Fuck her? Longarm coldcocked her, his right fist slamming against the shelf of her jaw while his left brushed the little Sharps aside.

Lenore reflexively jerked the trigger and the derringer spat smoke, flame, and a tiny bit of lead, but the bullet came nowhere near Longarm, winding up instead in one of the bedroom walls.

He plucked the Sharps from her fingers while Lenore was trying to recover her wits, and dropped the pistol into the pocket of his coat, which was lying nearby on the floor.

"Now, what the hell was that all about?" he demanded.

Lenore shook her head, trying to clear the cobwebs that muddied her thoughts. After a moment she spoke. "I like you, Custis. Please stay here today. Please. I . . . I need for you to."

"Why, dammit?"

"I am not the girl you thought I was. My name is not Lenore and I don't come from around here. Never mind who I am or where I'm from. That doesn't matter. What does matter is that you can't testify at that trial, Custis. Please. Promise me that. Don't go to court today."

"Willoughby hired you?"

"I don't know who hired me, Custis, and that is the truth. I was contacted . . . never mind by who. Whom? Who? I always get those mixed up."

"Never mind the English lesson. What are you supposed to do?"

"All I am required to do is to keep you from testifying. How I do it, whether I have to kill you or not, was left up to me." The girl began to cry. "I don't want to do that, Custis. Please don't make me."

Lenore reached under the bed again.

Longarm did not intend to wait and see what she brought out this time. He punched her again. Harder and square in the face.

Lenore's nose broke with an audible crunch. Her upper lip split open and spilled bright blood down over her tits, and she toppled over onto the floor at his feet, out cold this time.

If he'd had more time, he would have dragged the damn woman over to the Cheyenne city jail and booked her in on a charge of assault on a peace officer, but if he took time to do that he would surely miss the start of court. Lenore would have earned her pay after all.

Instead he hurriedly dressed, scowled at the sight of the naked girl on the floor—she was just beginning to stir with the return of groggy consciousness—and strode out of the empty house.

Whoever hired Lenore Bailey had a backup plan. Two men were waiting on the courthouse steps, one as far as he could get on either side of the doorway.

The men wore matching dusters. That was not particularly unusual, but the bulges that showed in the front of the dusters were. Either those two had the world's biggest hard-ons or they were hiding something else beneath the tan linen. And Longarm had a good idea what.

He shifted direction before he mounted the steps and walked nonchalantly to his right, as if unsuspecting and innocent.

The man closer to him pretended not to notice, although Longarm was sure the fellow would have a crawling sensation on the back of his neck, knowing that if he had to shoot he would have to swing the gun to his left, a difficult shift of aim for most men.

The other, of course, could confront Longarm face-on. Which meant he would have to be taken out first and his partner afterward.

Longarm drew his Colt, deliberately and with no hurry about it. Both gents in the linen dusters saw and reacted.

The one to the left of the doorway pointed something under his duster—a sawed-off shotgun as it turned out—but had no time to fire before Longarm's bullet smashed into his breastbone, taking first the breath away from him and then his life as he was launched backward against the stone building blocks.

The man on the right, much closer to Longarm, tried to swivel around before the lawman could get a second shot off.

He was late, and he damn well knew it. Instead of standing his ground to fire at the deputy who had already killed his partner, this one turned ghost pale and bolted for the wide open spaces.

Longarm thought about putting a bullet in the bastard's back, but there seemed no point to that. Instead he aimed a foot or so over the man's head and triggered a .45 slug. He would not have thought it possible, but the fellow managed to run even faster after that sizzler pinked the crown of his hat, sending the hat flying and the man flying even faster.

City police and sheriff's deputies came boiling out of the courthouse in response to the sudden gunfire, but Longarm's two shots had ended the conflict.

"What the hell . . . ?"

Longarm shrugged and reloaded his revolver. "I think somebody didn't want me to testify this morning. You boys want to take charge here? I'll give you my statement this afternoon, but right now I got me a date inside a certain courtroom."

James Willoughby, he noticed, looked almighty worried when he saw Longarm walk in unscathed. Had damn good reason to be worried too. It took no great powers of deduction to understand that Willoughby, or someone acting on his behalf, was behind these assaults.

Six hours later, with Longarm's testimony on the record and James Willoughby's jury deliberating the man's fate, Longarm returned to the house where he had left Lenore.

The front door was locked and no one answered his knock, so Longarm unfolded his pocketknife and jimmied the lock tongue.

There was no sign of Lenore—or whoever the hell she was—not that he'd really expected any. The narrow bed was there and the empty keg, but that was all that remained anywhere in the place.

Longarm went next door and rapped lightly on that door. After a minute or so and a repeat of the knocking, a man wearing bib overalls and a sleeveless shirt answered. He had a cup of coffee in one hand and a rather annoyed look on his face. Longarm guessed he'd interrupted the fellow's lunch.

"What is it?" the home owner growled. "Whatever it is, mister, I don't want to buy any." The gentleman's expression changed when Longarm displayed his badge. "Mister,

I done nothin'. You got to believe me about that."

"I believe you," Longarm assured him. "I got no beef with you. Just need to ask you a question or two."

The man grunted his assent, took a sip of the coffee, and scratched his crotch with the other hand.

"It's about the woman who lives next door. Or is renting there, I suppose."

"Woman? Mister, there ain't no woman over there. Hasn't been since Margarite died six, maybe seven years ago that was. Old Jules lived there by hisself until last October. His daughter came up from Omaha then and took Jules home with her to live. They sold off all his stuff. Auctioned it, they did. That was in December. I remember clear because I bought a right handsome thunder mug for my Mabel. Got it for fifteen cents and quite a bargain it was." He chuckled. "I gave it to my woman for Christmas, which is why I remember it so plain. The place has set empty ever since then."

"No one has had permission to live there?" Longarm withheld his opinion of a man who would give his wife a thunder mug for Christmas. And a used one at that.

"No." The fellow took another drink of his coffee, which in fact smelled tantalizingly good as Longarm still had not had time to get so much as a sip of the stuff all day. "No one there, though I hear tell the daughter will be putting the house up for sale. Jules won't be coming back here, I'm pretty sure. He'll likely stay with his girl until he dies."

"Thank you, sir. Sorry to have disturbed you, but you've been a big help."

The man grunted and withdrew, closing the door in Longarm's face.

Longarm grunted too. With disgust. He had been taken in by the girl, likely a high-priced whore from some big city, who called herself Lenore Bailey. Whoever she was, he was betting he would never see her again. If he happened to, he would arrest her.

But damn, she was a prime piece of tail.

He walked back to the courthouse, and beyond it to the café on the corner nearby. His belly was growling, and he was hoping he could induce the cook there to serve him up a platter of eggs and crisp bacon. Or ham. Maybe both. And coffee. Lordy, he did want some coffee now.

His mouth was already watering as he stepped inside the café.

Chapter 5

"Has the jury reached a verdict?"

"We have, Your Honor."

The judge turned his attention to the prisoner. "You will rise, sir."

"Fuck you," Willoughby snarled.

The judge did not argue the point. He did, however, nod to the deputies who were stationed in his courtroom. Without further direction, the deputies, big men both of them, walked over to Willoughby, took him by the arms, and lifted him bodily out of the chair where he had been insolently slouching.

"You may publish your findings," the judge said to the jury foreman.

"We find James Henry Willoughby guilty of the crime of murder," announced the foreman, a lanky chap whose accent suggested he was from Texas.

"Thank you, jurors." The judge turned his attention back to Willoughby, who still more or less dangled between the deputies. "James Willoughby, for the crime of murder, in which you shot down a man who was a far better person

than yourself, I sentence you to be hanged by the neck until
you are dead. A date for your execution will be determined
by the prison warden. Jurors, you are excused now. Deputies, you will take that sorry son of a bitch back to his cell
now, please."

Longarm grunted. It was a right and proper outcome. He
stood, reaching for a cheroot.

By habit he looked across the room for the girl with
the light brown hair, but of course there was no sign of her.
She likely would not be seen again, at least not by him.
Perhaps oddly, he hoped she had been paid for her services
in advance. Otherwise she would have gone to all that trouble for no purpose.

"Sir. Mister marshal, sir?" It was the old man again,
without his broom this time but just as quietly insistent that
he have a word with Longarm.

Longarm reached into his pocket and drew out a scant
handful of coins, some of which gleamed the yellow of
minted gold. He selected a quarter and held it out to the old
fellow, but the man shook his head.

"I ain't here to beg from you, Marshal. I got . . . I got
t'talk to you if you'd be so kind."

"Oh?"

"I need help, Marshal. That is, my grandbaby needs
your help. Can we talk, sir? Please?"

"Yes, I suppose so. Would you like some coffee while
we talk? We can go over to the café and—"

"Oh, no, sir, I couldn't go there, me being the local
drunk and you being a proper gentleman. There's folks
who . . . wouldn't take real well to me putting on airs."

"We could go to my room," Longarm suggested.

"But . . ."

"It's all right. I'm a deputy United States marshal, don't

forget. Nobody is going to stop me from talking to some-one who needs my help. Come along now." He smiled. "If you like, I can send a boy to fetch us coffee. Maybe some sandwiches."

The old fellow's eyes lit up, and he tried to stifle a laugh but failed. "I'd like that just fine, Marshal sir. Me in that hotel being waited on. Oh, yes, sir, I'd like that just fine. But if you don't mind, sir, it'd sit better with . . . with them folks if I didn't do it quite that way."

Longarm's eyebrows rose in inquiry. "Why not?"

"It would go hard on me afterward. I'll explain."

"I wouldn't want to cause you troubles."

"Tell you what I could do instead, Marshal. I could go fetch a tray with coffee on it. If anybody saw, they'd figure I was waiting on you an' that would be all right."

Longarm nodded. "That sounds reasonable. Let me give you some money then for the coffee. A sandwich too if you'd like. And don't worry. Whatever I spend will be on my ex-pense account. That means the government will end up pay-ing for it."

The old man grinned his appreciation of that idea and gladly accepted the fifty cents Longarm handed him.

Longarm started toward his hotel, then paused and turned to the old man. He extended his hand. "I'm Custis Long, but you can call me Longarm. All my friends do."

The old man eagerly accepted Longarm's handshake. "My name is Moses Arthur, Marshal, and I am right hon-ored to make your acquaintance, sir."

"Let's go then, Mr. Arthur." Longarm was very much aware of the hour. He was rapidly running out of daylight, and he still had to give a sworn statement to the Cheyenne police about those assholes that tried to shoot him earlier, and he had to wire Billy Vail to tell the marshal about the outcome of the trial. And about the fact that Longarm was available for another assignment now. He hoped this conversation with Moses Arthur about his grandchild would not take very long.

In fact, he had no idea how very long it would take.

Chapter 6

Longarm entered his room and by habit looked around before he relaxed. After all, Lenore and the second gunman were somewhere out there. It was not inconceivable that they might still want a piece of his hide.

The hotel room was empty, so Longarm removed his coat and hung it on a hanger in the wardrobe, tugged his string tie down from his throat, and unbuttoned his vest and the collar button on his shirt. He felt a helluva lot better after he did that.

He crossed to the front of the room, to a window overlooking the street in front of the hotel. The window was closed, so he raised the sash as far as it would go and the roller blind also. A faint breeze coming off the prairie that surrounded Cheyenne was more than welcome, the smell of coal smoke from the nearby railroad less so.

Moses Arthur would be along in a few minutes, but while he was waiting Longarm pulled the .45 from its leather, flicked the loading gate open, and punched out all five fat .45 cartridges from the cylinder.

Longarm always carried cleaning tools in his carpetbag.

He fetched it from the wardrobe and placed the bag on the bed so he could rummage inside for the cleaning rod, the two-ounce can of whale oil, and a greasy rag—carefully wrapped in oilcloth so it did not transfer any of the oil to his clothing—and proceed to clean the Colt, pulling the cylinder pin and dropping the cylinder out. He cleaned the bore first and held the revolver up to the light so he could see that the inside of the barrel was clean, then started working on the cylinder itself. He was midway through that familiar task when he heard a flurry of gunshots from the street below his window.

His Colt was inoperative at the moment, but his derringer was not. He palmed that, pulling it from his vest pocket, and hurried to the window. By the time he got there, the excitement was over except for the usual approach of pedestrians, shocked expressions on their faces. All of them seemed to be staring at something on the hotel steps. Longarm's view was blocked by the roof of the porch overhang, so he could not see exactly what the disturbance was all about.

There was no sign of the city police, so Longarm hustled down the staircase to the lobby and stepped out onto the porch, the derringer forgotten in his hand.

Moses Arthur lay there, sprawled in a pool of his own blood, a tray and two heavy chinaware coffee cups lying on the porch boards nearby. A man who was kneeling by his head looked up at the gun in Longarm's hand and said, "I know who you are, Marshal, but you aren't needed here now. This man is dead."

Longarm scowled. He shoved the little .41-caliber derringer back into his vest pocket and asked, "Did anyone here see what happened?"

One of the spectators stepped forward. "I did, sir."

Longarm grunted. "Tell me about it, please," he said.

"It was one man. He was following the drunk. They come across the street from down toward the café. He kinda hurried to get close, too close to miss his shot. Then he just pulled iron and put three into the old man's back. Deliberate, he was. Then he turned and walked away. Didn't even run. He walked down to the next block, got on a brown horse, and rode away just as pretty as you please."

"What did the man look like?" Longarm asked.

The fellow shrugged. "Just . . . you know . . . a man. Wore a gray hat. Side whiskers. I noticed that about him. Black coat and striped britches like about half the drovers that come through here. Wore his pistol down on the side of his leg, not like you carry yours. He looked, I dunno, maybe thirty years old. Maybe less."

"Have you see him in town before? Like maybe at the trial?"

The fellow shook his head. "No, sir. I sat through a good two days of that trial and I didn't see him in there."

"I did." Someone else spoke up.

"At the trial?" Longarm asked.

"No, sir. I seen him drinking at Jack Hanby's pub a couple nights this week. Might could be Jack knows him."

"Thanks. I'll ask," Longarm said. "Anybody else? Can anyone else add anything to what these gents said?"

But no one could. The Cheyenne police arrived and shooed the onlookers on their way.

Longarm went back upstairs to get his coat and, more importantly, his Colt, as soon as he finished cleaning and loading it. Then he went to city hall to give his statement to the police.

But what the *hell* had Moses Arthur wanted to tell him?

Chapter 7

"No, sir, I don't reckon I remember any such of a person," the barman at Hanby's Saloon said in response to Longarm's questions. "But then we get a lot of strangers passing through, this being the territorial capital and everything. Folks come in, stay a day or maybe a week while they get their business done, and then they're gone. We never see them again and don't pay any particular mind to the fact that they were here."

"I understand," Longarm told the man, "but it's important that I find this one."

The bartender shrugged. "I'd sure as hell help you if I could, Marshal. If someone says they saw the fellow drinking in here, then I'd say they likely did, but that don't mean that I remember him, for I don't."

"What about an old man named Moses Arthur?" Longarm asked.

"Oh, hell, everybody in Cheyenne knows old Mose."

"This fellow I'm asking about might've had words with Mr. Arthur sometime in the past few days," Longarm persisted.

"Now, I tell you true," the bartender said. "If somebody got into a fuss with Mose, I'd remember that for damn sure. Mose comes in here pretty much every night, panhandling the customers and such. We all tolerate the old fellow. He has a good heart, Mose does. No, I promise you I'd remember it plain if somebody gave Mose a hard time. The old man isn't good for much, but we all kinda like him, if you know what I mean."

Longarm grunted. "Did like him, you mean."

"Pardon?"

"Moses is dead. This fellow I'm asking about gunned him down this afternoon, three shots in his back from point-blank range."

The bartender whistled. "In the back? The son of a bitch! And you say Mose is dead now?"

"I'm afraid so," Longarm told him.

The barman turned and shouted, "Boys, them of you that hasn't heard, old Mose Arthur was killed today. I want you all to know that I'm setting a mug on the bar here. I expect everybody to ante up something to help pay for the old fellow's burying."

There were a fair number of patrons in the saloon at that evening hour. Nearly all of them crowded close so they could drop some money into the beer mug that the bartender set out for the purpose.

"Does anybody know if Moses had family in the area?" Longarm called out while the gents were in a charitable humor.

A skinny man who looked to be almost as old as Moses Arthur stepped forward. "I heard Mose talk about a daughter," the fellow said.

"From around here?" Longarm asked.

The man shook his head. "No, not here. Over . . . I think he said something about her living in Medicine Bow or . . ."

He shook his head again. "Someplace like that. I disremember exactly where he said."

"Does anybody know any reason why anyone would have it in for Mr. Arthur?" Longarm called out loud and clear.

No one did. But a well-dressed gentleman hung back when the crowd dispersed from around the burial mug. He approached Longarm and in a low voice said, "I don't know why all you people are getting so concerned about an old fart like Arthur. He wasn't a rung above being the town drunk, you know."

Longarm gave the man a long, cold stare. "What I *know*," he said, emphasizing the word, "is that Moses Arthur was attempting to convey information to a representative of the United States government. That old man was a witness who wanted to give testimony about something, an' that makes his death into the federal crime of tampering with a witness, an' if I have anything to say about it, that son of a bitch will be brought to justice for that an' for his other crimes as well."

The bar patron recoiled as if Longarm had slapped him. "I . . . I . . . Yes, sir," he stammered.

Longarm laid a nickel down for a beer he hadn't taken time to drink then turned on his heel and stalked out of Hanby's. There were a good many other saloons along the row in Cheyenne, and he wanted to hit them all to see if he could learn anything more about the old man who'd been shot in the back before he could have that promised word with Longarm.

Chapter 8

Longarm woke to a pounding headache and a vile taste in his mouth. He climbed out of bed feeling like he was a hundred years old and forced his eyes open. His eyelids felt like some son of a bitch must have crept in during the night and glued his eyes shut.

The floor was cold and gritty underfoot. He shivered, went over to the window, and closed it.

He fumbled inside his carpetbag until he found the bottle of rye whiskey he always carried with him. The hotel provided a drinking glass for its patrons. Longarm unfolded a paper of Mother Benedict's Headache Powder and dumped the contents into the glass, added an inch or so of the rye, and stirred it with his finger. He felt a little better after downing the slightly chalky mixture, although whether the improvement was due to the medicinal powder or to the whiskey he was not certain.

He poured a splash of water into the basin and rinsed his face with it, then dried with the rag the hotel provided by way of a towel. At least the cloth was clean; he had to give credit for that. He had stayed in places where sheets and towels were changed once a week or so.

On the other hand he had stayed in places where there simply were not any decent places. This was a hell of a lot better than that.

More or less revived, Longarm concluded that he did not feel like shaving himself this morning. The light was too poor and his hand . . . it would be better to go get a barbershop shave lest he slice his cheek wide open.

He ran a wet hand over his hair to slick it back—might as well get a haircut if he was going to be in the barber's chair anyway—and finished dressing.

A look at his watch suggested that he already missed the breakfast seating downstairs, so he would have to take care of that somewhere along the commercial strip too.

Longarm stepped out into the hall and pulled his door closed. There was no point in locking it, as it used a common skeleton key and could be picked by any kid with a hat pin.

He paused to look himself over in the hall mirror, then straightened his string tie and tipped his hat to a rakish angle. The combination of medicine and whiskey was beginning to make him feel much better.

The weather outside made him feel better yet. Practically chipper, in fact. The sky overhead was a deep, unblemished blue and the air was briskly refreshing, not chilled exactly but close to that. He breathed deep . . . and coughed until he thought his guts would come out. Deep breathing was not necessarily a good idea after a night of whiskey and cigars.

He tried again, not taking the air in quite so deeply this time, and grunted with mild dissatisfaction. The Cheyenne air smelled of coal smoke and clinkers because of the railroad, and of horse manure because of, well, the horse manure that lay drying in the streets.

But hell, a man cannot have everything. He was alive this morning, and that should be enough for the start of a new day. That thought reminded him that Moses Arthur was not among the living on this pleasant morning.

The old man died because of . . . what?

Longarm unconsciously hunched his shoulders and grimaced even as he made his way through the door of a restaurant a block and a half from the hotel.

By habit he chose a seat that placed his back to a wall. The menu was scrawled on a chalkboard hanging above the counter. When the waiter came, Longarm ignored the menu choices and ordered beefsteak and potatoes, both fried in tallow, and a slab of apple pie.

"Anything to drink?" the waiter asked.

"Coffee," Longarm told him, "hot as Hades and black as a whore's heart."

"Yes, sir, coming right up." The waiter turned away without bothering to write anything down. When he had gone, a seedy-looking fellow approached Longarm's table and sat down without invitation.

Longarm eyed the man with a hard stare. "I don't recall askin' you to set with me."

The man looked nervously over his shoulder then said, "I . . . I . . . I heard you talking. Last night. In Rupert's place."

Longarm had visited so damn many saloons the night before—and partaken of their whiskey—that he could not remember one called Rupert's. "All right. So?"

"So I . . . Maybe I know something about Mose."

Longarm's interest suddenly picked up. He leaned forward in his chair. "Go on."

"I . . . Listen, Marshal, I'm hungry. Could you stand me to a cup of coffee and something to eat?"

Longarm motioned for the waiter. "Give this man whatever he . . . Hell, just bring him the same as you're fixin' for me."

"Yes, sir." The waiter bobbed his head and withdrew.

Longarm lowered his voice and said, "All right, friend. Now, tell me what you know."

Chapter 9

Longarm followed the directions the old fellow had given him. A shack, he said. On the outskirts of town, out along the railroad tracks.

"You can't miss it," he had said, and in this case the man had been absolutely right about that. But not for the reasons he thought.

Moses Arthur's rickety shack was clearly visible because of the beacon of smoke that pointed the way to it. By the time Longarm got there, it was completely engulfed in flame.

A handful of men, all of whom looked like railroad workers, were carrying buckets of water from a nearby pump, but they had long since given up making any attempt to save Moses's place. Instead they were wetting down the walls and roofs of two nearby shacks where someone else was squatting.

The Cheyenne Municipal Fire Department showed up shortly after Longarm did, a dozen men hauling a water wagon with a rocker pump mounted on it. They deployed without too much confusion and were soon directing a stream of water onto what was left of Moses's place.

"Anybody know what happened here?" Longarm asked a soot-stained fellow wearing coveralls and a floppy rail-roader's cap.

"Far as I know, John over there was the first to see the fire. Hey, John. C'mere. This man wants to know what happened."

John looked to be barely out of his teens. He was dressed very much like the first fellow and was equally covered in soot and ash. "Yes?"

Longarm introduced himself and asked his question again.

John shrugged and said, "When I seen it, the front door was busted in an' smoke was coming out the back an' leaking out of the roof too."

"Could it have been a stove fire, do you think?" Longarm asked.

"Mose, he didn't have no stove in there. What little he cooked, just a potato now an' then or an ear of corn, he cooked in a fire pit around back. He found an old grate somewhere an' he cooked on that, never mind the time o' year or the weather. Mostly he didn't eat anything anyhow. He had a bad stomach. I guess that's why he was so scrawny-like. Well, that and the liquor. I think rotgut is mostly what he lived on."

"Did he smoke?" Longarm asked.

"He chewed a little, but he didn't smoke that I know of. Not that I know him all that well, mind you. It's just that I live over there," he pointed to a somewhat nicer shack closer to the town limits of Cheyenne, "so he passed by my place pretty regular. Sometimes we'd pass the time of day. You know how that is."

"Yes, I do," Longarm said. "You say the door to his place was busted when you first saw the fire?"

"That's right. It was busted clean open. One hinge was broken. The other hinge was a strip of leather tacked in place. That one held."

Longarm grunted, then asked, "Did you see anyone around when you first saw the smoke?"

John shook his head. "Not that I noticed."

By then the firemen had the fire under control. They pumped the rest of their water onto the charred remains of Moses Arthur's home, rolled up their hose, wheeled the fire cart around, then dragged it off toward whatever they used for a firehouse.

Longarm considered waiting for the ruined structure to cool enough that he could poke around inside, but there really was not much point. Whatever Mose might have had in there was gone now. Whatever secrets the old man wanted to impart were beyond salvaging. He was dead, and anything he might have hidden in his shack was burned up.

Longarm was scowling as he walked back to his hotel.

Medicine Bow, that man last night had said. Moses's daughter lived in or near Medicine Bow. Perhaps she knew what got her father killed.

It was worth a ride out there on the next westbound to find out. Longarm figured he owed the old man that much anyway. And whoever killed Moses Arthur had committed a federal crime when he interfered with a witness.

Not that Longarm knew just what Moses was a witness to, but still and all. It was a federal offense, and he had not only the right but a sworn duty to pursue the matter.

He lengthened his stride.

Chapter 10

"Say, you're the U.S. marshal, aren't you?"

Longarm stopped. He was on his way out of the hotel, carpetbag in hand. "I am. Do you need me for something?"

"I most surely do," the tall, neatly dressed fellow said. "I need to know who will pay for Moses Arthur's burial. I'm an undertaker, you see, and I have the old man laid out nice and peaceful with not a bullet hole in sight. But I need to know where to plant him and who will pay for it."

"What do you usually do when somebody dies a pauper?"

"We have a county-owned plot of ground. That's for folks with no family and no money left behind. But Moses had a daughter."

"You knew him well?" Longarm asked.

"Oh, no. I mean, everybody knew him, sort of. I saw him from time to time, but I never spoke to him that I recall."

"But you know he had a daughter?"

"Just from her letter. Girl named Netty."

Longarm set his carpetbag down on the hotel porch and tipped his Stetson back a mite. "Letter?"

"Sure. In his pocket," the undertaker said. "Naturally I

removed his clothes before I, um, worked on the corpse. Replacing fluids and so on. So I had to take his things off. The letter was in his pants pocket. Right front if you really want to know."

"Where is this letter now?"

"In my front room," the undertaker said.

"Wait here a minute while I put my bag inside. Then I want you to take me over to your office and show me that letter."

"Marshal, I don't mean to be pushy, but what I need to know is who will pay for the burying. I have expenses, you know. Professional fluids. A box. The hire of a laborer to open a grave. I have expenses."

"What does the county pay?"

"Only four dollars. That's barely enough to cover my direct cost. I was thinking . . . the federal government and everything . . . I was thinking you should pay six dollars for me to take care of Moses."

"I'm not authorized to commit the government of the United States to such an amount. But you can submit your request for payment to the attorney general's office in Washington City." Longarm struggled to suppress a grin when he said that. If this fellow waited for payment out of Washington for a request like this . . . The expression "until Hell freezes over" came to mind.

"You'll give me that address?"

"Be glad to," Longarm said, pulling a cheroot out of his inside coat pocket. "And you will give me the letter Moses was carrying, right?" He nipped the twist off the end of his cheroot, struck a match, and got his smoke alight.

"Yes. Yes, of course. Follow me, please."

The undertaker led the way with Longarm striding behind.

Chapter 11

"Medicine Bow. Next stop Medicine Bow. Ten minutes while we take on water. Medicine Bow. Next stop Medicine Bow. Ten minutes . . ." The conductor passed on through the car and beyond, delivering his message as he went.

The train began to slow, the cars clanking and clattering as their momentum caused each to crash into the coupling of the car ahead. Longarm waited until the train had slowed to a crawl before he stood and got his bag down from the overhead rack.

The mixed freight and passenger train stopped, backed up a few feet, stopped again, and inched forward as the engineer aligned the water sluice with the open receiver on the engine. Once he was sure the train was stopped for good, Longarm made his way down to the covered platform beside the tiny shack that served as the depot at Medicine Bow, Wyoming Territory. He was the only passenger who left the train at the little community.

Medicine Bow consisted of half a dozen or so businesses— two of those being saloons—and perhaps two dozen houses, plus what looked to be five or six acres of cattle pens and loading chutes.

Longarm displayed his badge to the fellow who served as both telegrapher and ticket seller inside the depot building. "Mind if I leave my bag here for a spell?"

"Be glad to oblige, Marshal, but you should know that I lock up at six. No one will be here until six tomorrow morning."

"Not even a telegraph operator?" Longarm asked.

The clerk, a young man who was struggling, with rather limited success, to raise a mustache crop under his nose, shook his head. "I'm all there is. Six days a week. I'm here from six to six." He grinned. "More or less."

"What happens if you get sick?"

"Then they send a relief operator down from Evanston. But that's only happened once. Was there something else I could do for you, Marshal?"

"No, that's fine. Thanks." Longarm started to turn away, then paused and asked, "Do you happen to know a woman named Netty?"

"Any idea what that would be short for?"

"No, sir," Longarm said. "All I know is Netty. Where do you get your mail here? Do you have a post office?"

"What we got is a postal contractor," the helpful clerk said. "That would be Seth Greaves, over to the grocery."

"The post office is in a grocer's store?" Longarm asked.

The clerk grinned and said, "Politics. Who knows who and all that sort of thing."

"Politics I understand," Longarm said. "You don't have to say more." He thanked the clerk and left the depot for the short, wide business street of Medicine Bow. Short because there just were not all that many businesses to accommodate, and wide because this was essentially a cow town with its commercial affairs coming from either the railroad or from cattlemen loading their beeves onto railroad cars. The animals needed plenty of room when they were hazed through town to the pens.

Greaves Greengrocers, Fine Meats and Seafoods was easy enough to find. The building was a large, two-story clapboard affair with a sign over the porch overhang declaring all the wonderful things Seth offered to his customers. Including in smaller print at the bottom of the sign, UNITED STATES POST OFFICE.

Longarm crossed the wide street and walked the half block west to Greaves's store.

A middle-aged man with a paunch and a splendid mustache that must surely have been the envy of the young railroad clerk greeted the newcomer. "Afternoon, sir. How can we help you today?"

We? There was no one else visible in the store. But perhaps, Longarm thought, the man had a mouse in his pocket.

He approached the counter and again displayed his badge. Seth Greaves stood a little straighter and took on a more serious expression when he saw that. "Yes, Marshal?"

"I'm lookin' for a woman . . . I don't know how old . . . who goes by the name of Netty. I figure if she lives anywhere around here she'll be getting her mail through you, so mayhap you would know who she is and where I can find her."

Greaves frowned in thought for a moment, then shook his head. "I don't have any patrons with that name. Sounds like somebody's pet name though. Any idea what it'd be short for?"

"No, sir, I don't," Longarm admitted.

"Important that you find her?"

"Yes, it is."

"Got a last name?" Greaves asked.

"No, sir. Far as I know, that could be it."

"Well I can tell you certain sure that we got no postal patrons with Netty for a last name. If you could give me the right first name, I might be able to put a last name with it, but I'd have to have more than just the nickname."

"All right," Longarm said. "How about the last name Arthur?"

Greaves shook his head. "Sorry. I don't know of anyone with that name, but if you think of anything else, I'd be proud to help you," he said.

Longarm touched the brim of his Stetson by way of a thank-you and went back outside.

With only that name to go on, finding Moses Arthur's Netty might not be as simple as Longarm had hoped.

Chapter 12

Longarm checked his Ingersoll. There might yet be enough time for him to find Mose Arthur's Netty—He just did not know where to look.

What he did know was that someone had had a reason to murder the old man. Good, bad, or just plain stupid—there was a reason behind it. Longarm wanted to know that reason, first because Arthur had been a potential witness before a federal peace officer, and second, perhaps even more compelling, because the murder had taken place practically under his nose, which just plain offended the shit out of Deputy United States Marshal Custis Long. That was the long and the short of it.

Mindful that the railroad depot would close in a few hours, he headed down the street, and turned in at the first of Medicine Bow's two saloons.

It was nearly dark inside the place and cool after the heat of the sun. The scents were pleasantly familiar. Sawdust and suds. The yeasty smell of beer and the sharper smell of cheap whiskey. Traces of perfume hung in the air too, suggesting that a man could buy more than a drink in the place.

Longarm suspected the saloon would be a beehive of activity once the beef shipping season got under way. Now, however, there was only a portly man wearing a no-longer-white apron and one customer propped up on the brass rail that ran in front of the bar.

"What can I get you, mister?"

"Got rye whiskey?"

"Course I do. Glass or a bottle for you, friend?"

"Just a glass will do me, thanks." Longarm dug out a quarter and got back a small glass of golden rye and ten cents change.

The bartender slid a bowl of peanuts down the bar so Longarm could reach them, and said, "Funny thing. Two strangers in one day. Cowhands and cattle buyers we get, but not generally two strangers passing through."

"How do you know I'm not a buyer?" Longarm asked.

The bartender shrugged. "You don't got the look. Besides, it isn't the time of year for the buyers to come in."

"Ship a lot of beef out of here, do they?" Longarm asked, taking up his rye. He held the glass under his nose to take in the scent, then allowed a small quantity of the whiskey to trickle past his lips, held it on his tongue for a moment before he swallowed. Damn, but it was good.

"I have a question if you don't mind," Longarm said.

"Sure. Anything."

The other patron tapped his mug on the bar, and the bartender held a finger up to Longarm. "Just a moment."

Longarm nodded and took another small sip. After his overindulgence in Cheyenne, he wanted to go slow with the liquor this time.

The barman plucked the empty mug off the bar, tugged on a tap, and filled it. Longarm noticed that he let the suds overflow so that the mug was filled to the rim with dark, foaming beer. Full measure. The deputy U.S. marshal liked that. The bartender came back to stand in front of him. "Now, what is that question?"

"I'm lookin' for someone named Netty. That's all I know. Just Netty. Would you know anyone like that?"

"Now, that is the strangest damn thing," the bartender said. "Remember I said you're the second stranger in town today? Well that other fella asked the same question. He's looking for somebody called Netty too."

"What did you tell him?"

The man shrugged. "Same thing I got to tell you. I don't know anybody by that name."

"Shit," Longarm grumbled.

"Have you asked Sam Greaves over at the post office?"

Longarm nodded. "That was my first stop. Mr. Greaves said the name was new to him. Now, I'm thinking it must be a nickname. Something like that."

"Excuse me," the man standing nearby said. He was tall, with full whiskers but neatly trimmed, and he was not dressed like a saddle bum. Did not look much like a town merchant either. His voice was friendly enough though. Very polite.

"Do you want a refill already, Chuck?" the barman asked.

"No, I'm still good here. I was talking to that other fellow."

"Me?" Longarm asked.

"That's right. You asked about somebody called Netty, right?"

"I sure did."

The man moved closer, dragging his mug with him. He took a peanut out of the bowl and carefully took the meat out of the shell, his fingers busy with that task while he spoke. "I heard such a name," he said.

Longarm's interest quickened.

"I'm trying to remember where that would've been."

"Would it help your memory if I was to set you up to a drink?" Longarm asked.

The fellow smiled. "I'm not trying to cadge drinks off of you, mister. I can buy my own. No, I'm really trying to recall . . ." He snapped his fingers and grinned. "Now I recollect. It was out at the Birdwell ranch. The missus was saying something to her hired help. Called her Netty. I never heard what her right name might be, but I'm sure about that much."

The bartender tipped the bottle of rye over Longarm's glass to refill it and said, "If Chuck says it, you can take that to the bank. I've never known him to be wrong."

"I wouldn't go that far," Chuck said modestly. "It's just that I get around a lot. Meet plenty of folks. Pretty much everybody around here actually."

"That's the truth," the barman injected. "Chuck here is a vet'rinarian. Doctors just about every horse or cow in the county."

"Only those that need it," Chuck said. "I keep trying to find a way so I can charge my fees for every animal, but for some reason the cattlemen don't much cotton to that idea." He laughed and took a deep pull on his beer.

"I'd be happy to buy you another of those," Longarm offered.

"Thanks, but I have to go. There are some sick sheep over south a way."

"Before you go, would you mind pointing me to this Birdwell place you mentioned?"

"I'll be glad to. Step outside with me and I'll tell you how to get there." He looked at the bartender and nodded, "Thanks, Jerry. I'll see you this evening, right?"

"Right," the barman said, taking Chuck's mug down from the bar and dropping it into a basin of soapy water. Longarm noticed that he left the glass of rye where it was, rather than assume Longarm would be leaving after he got directions to the Birdwell ranch. Longarm definitely liked this place.

"Now about this Birdwell place . . . ?" He followed Chuck out onto the boardwalk that fronted the saloon.

Chapter 13

It looked like he would not be in and back out of Medicine Bow in one day, but duty trumped comfort in Longarm's view, so he retrieved his carpetbag from the railroad depot and asked the clerk there where he could put up for the night.

"Oh, we got a hotel. It isn't much of a place, but it serves the purpose. Cheap this time of year too. When the buyers are in and the cattlemen are shipping, that's another story entirely. The price goes up, but the place fills up anyhow. Let me tell you how to get to it," the clerk offered.

Five minutes later Longarm was standing at the counter of a small and rather shabby hotel a block off the wide main street.

"Will you be staying long?" a skinny kid with freckles and big teeth asked. Probably the proprietor's son, Longarm guessed.

"No idea," Longarm told him. "When I leave, I'll give you a voucher for payment."

The kid scowled. "I don't think we can do that."

"Sure you can. It's a U.S. government pay voucher. Good as gold anywhere."

"I'll have to ask my mom about that."

"Fine, but in the meantime just give me my room so I can get on about my business."

"I suppose I can do that." The youngster turned toward the board where a dozen or so keys were hanging on small nails. "Front room or back?" he asked.

"Whichever is quieter," Longarm said.

"That would be in the back then. We sometimes get some rowdy folks in the streets. Not so much right now, but there are times." He took a key down from the wall and handed it to Longarm. "Room four," he said. "Upstairs in the back. Do you want me to carry your bag up for you?"

Hoping for a tip, Longarm thought. "No, thanks. I got it." He accepted the key and thanked the boy.

Going up the stairs in the ramshackle little hotel was one of the more dangerous things he had done lately, he was sure. The steps were warped and creaked alarmingly when he put his weight on them. He stayed close to the banister so he would have something to grab on to should one of the treads give way underfoot. As it happened he was able to reach the top without plunging to his death. That was a relief until he remembered that he would have to take those same steps to get down again.

Room number four was tiny, with a narrow iron bedstead and a small washstand that held a basin and an empty pitcher. There was a thunder mug beneath the bed. Hooks on the wall served in place of a wardrobe. Still, the room was spotlessly clean, the pillow fluffy, and the sheets smelling—he sniffed them to be sure—of laundry soap and sunshine. He had stayed in far worse places than this.

Longarm deposited his bag by the foot of the bed and immediately hazarded the staircase again. The kid was sitting on a ladder-back chair in what passed for a lobby, a book open in his lap and a pad on foolscap and a sharp pencil in his hand.

"Studying something?" Longarm asked.

The boy smiled. "Yes, sir. I'm going to be an engineer. Come fall, I'll be away to college."

"Good for you, son. Your mom must be proud of you."

The boy shrugged. "Truth is she's kind of mad about it. I won't be here for the fall shipping, so she'll have to take on hired help."

Longarm grinned. "Hired with actual money, is that it?"

"Yes, sir. But I'm set on what I want. I'm going to lay track and build bridges. I'm going to build wonderful things."

"With that kind of attitude, you will indeed do those things," Longarm said. "Not to change the subject, but could you tell me where I can hire a horse?"

"Yes, sir. There's a livery just one street over and three blocks down." He pointed.

Longarm hadn't thought the town big enough to *have* three blocks in any direction, but apparently he was wrong about that. "Thank you, son. Sorry I disturbed your studies." He touched the brim of his Stetson and strode out of the little hotel in search of that livery barn.

Chapter 14

Longarm wasn't sure if he had walked into a livery stable or a social club. There were five old men sitting on chairs that looked like they must have come from a trash heap. Two of them were playing checkers. All were scratching their whiskers and spitting tobacco juice. Longarm smiled. It is a good thing to have friends.

"Gentlemen," he said, touching the brim of his Stetson and bowing his head in deference to their ages.

"What can we do you for, sonny?" one of the checkers players asked.

"Need t'hire a horse," Longarm told him.

"Cash money?"

"As good as. I can offer you government scrip."

"What are you, a surveyor or something like that?"

"Deputy U.S. marshal," Longarm said.

The old fellow grunted and stood, unfolding a lean and lanky frame. He was bowlegged and bewhiskered and looked old enough to have been neighbors with Methuselah. "I expect a U.S. marshal ain't likely to cheat me. All right then. Let me show you what I got. Billy, don't you be mov-

ing any of my pieces there. I know where ever' damn one
of them sets, and if you try and cheat me I'll take a strop
and whup your ass." He turned his attention back to Longarm and said, "This way."

They went behind the barn, to a set of corrals. A dozen
head or so of tall, handsome mules were there. So were
three broad-rumped horses. "Take your pick," the old man
said.

"You know 'em," Longarm said. "I'll trust your judg-
ment."

The old boy took a catch rope down from a peg on the
barn wall and deftly shook out a small loop. As easy as if
he were tossing a pebble, he made his throw. The loop
dropped neatly over the head of a seal brown that was built
like a bulldog, broad in both rump and chest and with a
good forty-five-degree angle on the shoulder, suggesting a
reasonably comfortable trot. Not that any trot is really comfortable.

He bypassed a much more handsome—or anyway much
flashier—black and a tall, red roan in favor of the rather
drab brown horse. "You got anything against riding a mare,
Marshal?"

"No, sir. Not unless she's in season."

"This one ain't. She rides good and she's steady."

"If you recommend her, that's good enough for me,"
Longarm said. "I'll be needin' tack on her too. I didn't ex-
pect t'need a saddle this time out, so I left mine back in
Denver."

The old man cackled. "Helluva town, Denver. I been
there a couple times. Can't hold a candle to San Francisco,
though, when it comes to raising hell. You ever been to San
Francisco, Marshal?"

"I have," Longarm said with a nod.

"Got me some fine memories in San Francisco." His

grin widened. "Denver too for that matter. And Evanston. Why, I could tell you some things. . . . You ever smoke any of that opium stuff? I tell you true, Marshal, a pipe of that shit and a couple of those little China girls they got over there and a man could think he'd died and gone to Heaven."

While he was jabbering on, the old fellow was busy selecting a saddle from several hung on racks inside the barn, taking down and sorting out a bridle and reins, then getting the blocky little mare tacked up and ready to ride.

"I'm gonna be charging you a dollar a day for the horse and fifty cents for the gear," he said when he handed the reins to Longarm. "You take care with this little girl and bring her back sound when you're done with her. We can settle up then."

Longarm adjusted the stirrups, gauging the length against his arm, then stepped into the saddle.

The brown stood steady but stepped out nicely with a touch of the heel.

Longarm touched the brim of his hat to the old fellow again as he rode away from the livery.

Now, if he could just find this Netty person, maybe he could get a handle on why Moses Arthur was murdered.

Chapter 15

Longarm judged he was about halfway out to the Birdwell place when a bullet whined past his face. Seconds later he heard the sound of the shot. By that time he had reined the brown to a halt and turned, intending to shout at the simpleton whose careless shot came so near.

It was only then that he discovered the shot was not a careless one. It was deliberately calculated to kill.

A second bullet followed that first but was as poorly aimed as the other had been. This slug struck the brown mare in the side of the head. She dropped instantly, taking Longarm down with her.

He kicked free of the stirrups before the dying horse hit the ground. He rolled away, then scuttled back again so he could hunker down behind the horse's body.

His Colt was in his hand although he had no conscious memory of drawing it.

A wisp of white smoke hanging in the air above an outcropping of gray granite showed him clearly enough where the shots had come from, but the distance was impossibly far for a handgun.

A little too far for a rifle too, at least for a rifle aimed by whoever it was who shot at him. Obviously the shooter was not a marksman.

A really good shot might have been able to score a solid hit at that distance. Longarm estimated it to be a little more than two hundred yards. That range was certainly doable with something like a .50-100 buffalo gun, but with a .44 cartridge in a saddle carbine, a cartridge designed to be used in revolvers, shooting at that distance was a matter of wishes and luck.

This time the luck was on Longarm's side.

He lay there, tight against the seat of the saddle where he would be protected, waiting for the shooter to come down to admire his handiwork, but that did not happen. Instead the sun sank lower and lower, eventually striking Longarm directly in the eyes.

And then it was gone, taking the lingering daylight with it. Once the light was gone the night chill settled in. Longarm shivered and, disgusted, shoved his Colt back into leather.

The shooter, whoever he might have been and whyever he wanted a deputy United States marshal dead, was long gone now, and Longarm had not gotten so much as a brief glimpse of him.

Longarm stood, leaned down, and brushed himself off, then set about the rather unpleasant task of pulling the old liveryman's saddle and bridle off the dead horse.

Chapter 16

Longarm's feet hurt. Hurt like hell, in fact. He hated to think how they would have felt had he been wearing the tall heels and high arches of the boots normally favored by cowhands and wranglers. His cavalry boots were intended to allow troopers to fight dismounted and thus made the pain considerably less than it might have been.

Even so . . . his feet hurt like hell, and he would have been very pleased to one more time run up against the bastard who shot at him.

Longarm was not striding out quite as comfortably as he had to begin with and his feet were kicking up dust, as he made his way up the lane from the gate to the Birdwell place. It was just as had been described to him back in Medicine Bow: a set of tall gateposts with a board mounted overhead. There was just enough light from the stars and moon to let him make out the stylized bird burned into the board, flanked by Flying B brands on either side.

The ranch headquarters consisted of a large and handsome two-story main house, barns and sheds on one side of the ranch yard, and the cookhouse and a low-roofed bunkhouse on the other side. Longarm wearily headed for the owner's home.

No lights showed anywhere on the place. But then it was probably well past midnight now. Sensible folks would be abed.

Longarm mounted the steps onto a porch that ran across the front of the Birdwell house. He chose a wicker-back rocking chair and settled into it, tipping his hat over his eyes and crossing his arms. With any sort of luck he should be able to catch a little sleep before the family—and perhaps this mysterious Netty—woke up.

Longarm heard stirrings inside the house before any lights came on. Through the open window close to his rocking chair he could smell a hint of baking bread and coal smoke. Obviously the Birdwell cook was up and busy.

He stood, his knee cartilage popping, and carefully made his way down the steps in the near-dark of an approaching dawn. He was fairly proud of himself; he only tripped twice as he went around to the back of the house.

There was a small utility porch on the back with a stand and washtub and—amazingly—a hand pump where the cook and washwoman could draw water. Longarm could see a little better by the time he got to the back of the house, either because his eyes were better adjusted or because of the increasing light. He climbed the three steps onto the porch and lightly knocked on the back door.

Moments later the door was opened and light flooded the utility porch. "*Sí?*"

Longarm frowned. No one had suggested that his missing Netty was Mexican.

"Are you called Netty, ma'am?" He would have said it in Spanish but could not recall how to do that. After a few seconds he snapped his fingers in annoyance with himself and said, "*Es su nombre Netty?*"

The cook shook her head and answered, "*Mi nombre es Maria.*"

"Shit," Longarm mumbled.

Maria raised her eyebrows.

"No, not . . . not you, ma'am. Mr. Birdwell. Can I see Mr. Birdwell, please?"

Haltingly, Maria said, "The mister he not up."

"When he gets up, when he's awake, tell him there is a deputy United States marshal out here that needs to see him." The words sailed completely over the woman's head, but when Longarm produced his badge and showed it to her, her eyes went wide and she grabbed a handful of apron and skirt before whirling around and dashing inside the house.

The back door remained open, and Longarm could hear Maria's footsteps pounding on a staircase somewhere inside.

He leaned against the door frame—it had been a long and tiring night—and waited. Quickly, very quickly, a tall man with a mop of unkempt gray hair appeared.

"What is this about you putting Maria under arrest?" he asked.

Longarm chuckled. Then explained. Birdwell turned his head and called out something in Spanish that was much too rapid for Longarm to follow. Then he opened the door wide and said, "Come inside and have some breakfast with us. My wife may be able to help you. She will be down as soon as she is dressed. In the meantime you and I can have some coffee."

Longarm smiled. "I can't tell you how good that sounds." He removed his Stetson and stepped inside Maria's kitchen.

Chapter 17

"I had just cause to fire her and that is all I shall say on the subject," Ophelia Birdwell said, her chin high and lips primly compressed. Mrs. Birdwell was a rather stern woman and—Longarm sought a way to think of her charitably—not handsome. She was, in fact, homely. Figure like a beer barrel and a face that would stop clocks. Longarm marveled that Birdwell could abide waking up to that sight.

Of course it was always possible that Mrs. Birdwell was a great asset to her husband. The poor sap might be getting up before dawn and sneaking out of the bedroom so he did not have light to see by. Imagining this woman naked . . . Longarm shuddered at the thought.

He raised his cup and took a swallow of the coffee, reached for another biscuit and the honey pot. Biscuits and honey. By themselves not a bad way to start the day, and this meal included pork chops and fried potatoes too. He finished his third chop and, stuffed, pushed his plate away. He even refused Maria's attempt to refill the coffee.

"I'm full t'the top and thank you both," he said. "You been most kind."

"Sorry we couldn't help you," Birdwell said. "The hands will be ready to ride out by now. My foreman is a man named Jess Moore. Tell him you're to have a horse to get you back to town. Just leave it at the livery and one of us will pick it up the next time we're in."

"That's might nice of you," Longarm said. He meant it quite sincerely. He had expected it, of course, but it was not something Birdwell was required to do. "I got one of the livery's saddles back there by the dead horse, so if you'll give me the loan of a bridle an' bit, I'll ride your animal bareback that far."

"Fine. Tell Jess what you need. He'll fix you up." Birdwell checked his watch and added, "You should go find him now before he rides out."

"Yes, sir, and thank you again for your help." Longarm bowed to the lady of the house and added his thanks to her too.

Ophelia Birdwell sniffed—he suspected that expressed the woman's attitude toward many things in her life—and nodded acceptance of his gratitude. Lordy, he could not imagine . . . He shook his head to clear away that sort of thinking. Shit, the mere thought of fucking Ophelia could put a man off sex for weeks. Months, maybe.

"Please to excuse me, folks." Longarm turned and left, by the front door this time.

Feeling considerably better than when he'd walked into the yard, he ambled over to a corral where half a dozen hands were saddling their mounts in anticipation of the day's work. These boys had it easy. It was already full daylight and they were just now getting started. A good many outfits had their hands riding out in darkness. Getting back after dark too, some of them.

"Hello, mister," one of the men said as he pulled on the

cinch of a short coupled horse the color of mustard. "Where'd you come from?"

Longarm ignored the question and asked one of his own. "Which one of you is Moore? The boss sent me to find him."

The cowhand shot his jaw in the direction of a gangly, balding man with a scraggly mustache and legs that were bowed so wide a calf could likely run through them without touching on either side. "That's Jess."

"Thanks." Longarm went over to the ranch foreman and introduced himself.

Moore appeared to be skeptical about turning one of his horses over to a stranger, so Longarm explained his mission, but only mentioned losing the livery horse. He did not explain how.

"All right. If the boss says so." He turned his head and shouted, "Lafferty. Rope out that gray that Petey rode yesterday. This gentleman is gonna take it to get back to town. Put a bridle on it but no saddle."

The man named Petey nodded, tied his horse to a fence post, and went back into the corral.

Moore looked back to Longarm and said, "Did you find out what you need to know about Netty?"

"No, not really. Mrs. Birdwell just said she was fired for cause. She didn't say what cause."

Moore chuckled. "I'll just damn well bet you she didn't."

"Sounds like there's a tale that I should be knowin' about this," Longarm said.

"Yeah, but it ain't one that you'll hear spoken about inside that house," Moore said with a nod toward his employer's handsome home.

"And that tale would be . . . ?"

"Netty is no spring chicken, but she's a handsome woman, no doubt about it." He laughed. "The boss, he thought so too. He got to tapping some of that. Getting it right regular, I guess, until the battle-axe walked in on the two of them one evening when she was supposed to be asleep in bed. The way I hear it, she woke up and was thirsty, so she went downstairs to tell Netty to fix her tea and a snack. She went into Netty's room off the kitchen there, and what does she see but Jim Birdwell's hairy ass humping up and down and Netty underneath him squeaking and squealing like she always done." Moore's grin got wider. "That was the last of Netty on this place. Damn near the end of Jim too. I'll bet he hasn't had a piece of ass since Netty got thrown off the place."

Longarm chuckled and said, "It sounds like you know something about how Netty acts when someone is in the saddle with her."

Moore shrugged. "She's a good woman. Don't mistake that, Marshal. It's just that she likes men. Likes to please. And she isn't selling it. It's more like with her it's, um, a *friendly* thing, I suppose you could say."

"Any idea where I could find her now?" Longarm asked.

"Oh, hell yes." He laughed. "Soon as Coon Morgan heard she was available, he hired Netty to cook for him and his two hands."

"Coon?"

Moore nodded. "You'll understand the name soon as you see Coon. He has these dark, dark circles around both his eyes. Makes him look like a raccoon. I think he's been called that since he was a pup. I got no idea what his right name would be. All I ever heard him called was Coon."

"Can you tell me how to get to his place?" Longarm asked.

"Easy as can be," Moore said as the hand named Petey led a barrel-chested gray horse out of the corral and gave its reins to Longarm. "What you do is to go over this way . . ."

Chapter 18

Longarm needed to go to Coon Morgan's ranch so he could speak with Netty, but he needed that saddle first, so he detoured back along the road to Medicine Bow until in the distance he could see the carcass of the livery stable's brown mare.

The dead horse was barely visible under a moving blanket of magpies and buzzards. But then in nature nothing goes to waste. Less than a day after the mare was killed she was about half-eaten. A few more days and there would be nothing left but bones. And the coyotes would soon scatter those all to hell and gone.

Longarm sat balanced atop the borrowed gray for some time while he studied the country in a broad circle, with the brown's carcass at the center.

Whoever it was that shot at him yesterday could well have returned to plan another ambush, with the saddle and bridle as bait that Longarm could be expected to return to. If there was a trap, Longarm had no desire to walk into it.

He sat and watched for the length of time it took him to smoke a cheroot, then he rode the rim of that imaginary circle, staying a quarter mile or so out from the mare and examining every rock, shrub, and cactus that might conceal a man with a rifle. He found nothing, but only when a very careful search was concluded did he rein the gray gelding toward the dead horse.

A dark cloud of flapping, squawking, fluttering birds filled the air as Longarm's approach frightened them away from their meal.

By the time he threw his leg over the gray's neck and slid down to the ground, he was damned glad to be standing on his own hind legs again. Riding bareback just was not as comfortable as being able to relax in a good stock saddle.

It took only moments for him to saddle the gray. He hung the mare's bridle on the saddle horn, put his foot in the stirrup, and mounted. Damn but it felt good to have leather between him and the horse, and it felt even better to have stirrups to take his weight instead of having to use his thigh muscles constantly.

"Now then," he muttered aloud, "let's see can we find Coon Morgan's place now that I've gotten away from the track Jess Moore pointed out for me."

The gray horse twitched its ears at the sound of his voice.

Man and horse were not fifty yards from the brown mare's carcass before the carrion eaters began to return.

Chapter 19

Coon Morgan had a rawhide outfit with a long, low dugout for a ranch headquarters and three more smaller dugouts that likely served as a bunkhouse and storage. An adobe brick oven stood beside a pavilion, a shake roof supported on four tall posts. A long table sat beneath the roof of the pavilion, and there was a raised fire pit with an iron grill over it at the end opposite the brick oven.

A set of corrals, haystacks, and sorting pens lay beyond the dugouts. Half a dozen horses stood, hipshot and tails switching, close to a partially filled hay bunk.

It was past midday when Longarm rode into the yard. Smoke rose from the oven, and there was a woman bending over a washtub stirring clothes with a long wooden paddle. The tub sat well off the ground, resting on more adobe bricks. She had a fire built beneath the tub to boil her wash water.

Longarm stopped the gray horse short of the woman and her washing so as not to billow any dust over her clean clothing. At his approach she set the paddle aside and waited to see what this newcomer wanted.

Longarm remained in the saddle while he touched the brim of his Stetson. "Ma'am." He nodded.

"Hello." She was a handsome woman, he noticed. Tall but with a good figure. Gray hair pulled back in a bun. At the moment she was not displayed to best advantage as she was red-faced and sweaty from working over the boiling water. Wisps of hair strayed from her bun, and her apron was smudged with ash and soot. Still and all, she had strong features and pale gray eyes that were strikingly intense.

"My name is Custis Long, ma'am, deputy U.S. marshal outa Denver. I'm lookin' for a lady named Netty."

"Good Lord!" she blurted. "Have I done something wrong?"

"Are you Netty?"

"I'm Elizabeth Whorle," she said. "Most everyone calls me Netty. Always have."

"May I step down, ma'am? I'd like to talk to you."

She took a double handful of apron and wrung the cloth as if trying to squeeze water from it. "Mercy," she said. "I've forgot my manners. Yes, please, do get down. Are you hungry, Marshal? Can I get you something to eat?"

"I could eat," he said. Breakfast at the Birdwell place had been a good many hours—and miles—ago, and while of course he could stand to wait until he got back to Medicine Bow for his supper, he really would rather not. "You're mighty kind, miss."

"Just call me Netty." He wasn't sure, but he thought she might be making eyes at him. "Sit down at the table there, Marshal. I'll find you a bite and then we can talk."

He led the gray over to the corral and tied it there, then stopped at a pump that he hadn't been able to see when he rode in, the well being on the far side of the main dugout from where he had been. He moistened his handkerchief and used it to cool his face and mop some of the trail dust off his neck, then washed his hands and went back around to the front, where Netty had coffee, a plate, and a knife and fork waiting for him.

She was nowhere in sight, but she quickly appeared, hurrying out of the small dugout that he had assumed—correctly, it seemed—was the cookhouse. She bore a platter of small steaks swimming in dark gravy, a bowl of turnips, and a basket that held freshly baked bread and a bowl of sweet butter.

"Ma'am," he told her, "you do know how to please a man."

"Do you think so? Marshal, you don't know the half of it. But we can leave all that to later. Right now sit down and fill your belly. When you've had your dinner, we can talk."

Chapter 20

"I'm here," he said around a mouthful of bread sopped in gravy, "because of a man named Moses Arthur. I have reason to believe that you might've known him."

"Known him? Good Lord, I would hope so. After all, he *is* my father." She laughed and shook her head. "He must have gotten himself into an awful mess this time if there is a U.S. marshal come all the way out here to find me. But really, sir, there is not a bad bone in his dear body. It is just that he gets . . . indignant, I suppose you would call it. About any sort of wrongdoing. Then when he gets drunk, he spouts off about whatever his latest peeve is. But I promise you, whatever this is about, he means no harm. So tell me. What is it this time?"

Longarm laid his fork aside, wiped his mouth with the napkin she had given him, and cleared his throat before he went on. "Your father, you say."

"That's right. And a very sweet man," Netty said.

"Then I have the very unpleasant duty to tell you, miss, that your father was murdered a few days ago. Shot down on the streets of Cheyenne."

Netty's expression crumbled from one of amused tolerance to one of painful sorrow. "Oh, my. Murdered. I cannot imagine . . ." She began to very quietly weep. "I always thought . . . I mean he was old and everything and he drank and . . . Murdered!"

Longarm stood and put an arm around her shoulders. Netty pressed her face against him. He could feel tremors of shock and pain course through her body. He stroked her back in an attempt to comfort her. The close contact and perhaps Netty's vulnerability combined to give him a hard-on, and he had to twist slightly away to keep her from feeling his dick dig into her belly. After a minute or so her sobbing subsided and she stepped back. Longarm quickly sat back down again so the tabletop would hide the protrusion that threatened to burst the buttons of his fly.

"Sit down. Please," he said, motioning to the bench across the table from where he sat. "Can I get you something? Some of that coffee maybe?"

Netty nodded. "Thank you."

Dammit, he thought. He hadn't been thinking when he just automatically made that offer. The gesture was genuine, but the result . . . she was sure to see the front of his trousers poking out.

Fretting about that fortunately began to relieve the problem. He stood and got the coffeepot and another mug for Netty to use.

"I'm sorry to've put that on you so blunt, miss. It's just that your name . . . a married name, of course. I should've thought."

She wiped her eyes with the hem of her apron, took a deep breath, and peered down into the coffee in her mug. After a moment she looked up again, her eyes meeting Longarm's. "Tell me about it, please. And why would a United

States marshal be involved if he was killed in Cheyenne like you say."

"Moses was working at the courthouse," he said. "I was there for a trial. He approached me. Said he had information. He didn't say what except that it involved his grandchild. Apparently he thought that this, whatever it is, was something that a U.S. marshal should be told about rather than the town or county authorities. Moses was on his way to meet with me about it when he was killed. Tampering with a federal witness is a federal offense, which gives me jurisdiction. Besides, he was my witness an' that just pissed me off if you will excuse the language, Miz Whorle."

Netty's right hand crept up to her throat, and she looked like she might begin to cry again. "Daddy wanted to talk with you about my little girl, Marshal."

"Your daughter? That would be the grandchild he meant, I suppose."

"It has to be, since Justine is his only grandchild."

"Justine Whorle?"

"Justine Crowne. Carl Crowne was my first husband. John Whorle was my third. Well, I called him a husband. Common law, you understand. But Carl and I were married in a church, all legal as could be. Justine, she was living with Carl's parents on a place down near Baggs. They are old folks, almost as old as Daddy, but they were good to her. Good for her too. I know that. I'm . . . The truth is that I've never been much of a mother. Wasn't much of a daughter either, I suppose. But I love Justine with all my heart. I want you to know that. It's just that it was better for her to live in a proper way, not like me. And the truth is that, well, Justine and I have been estranged. I haven't seen nor heard from her in two years or more."

"Obviously your father was in touch with her somehow

or with her other grandparents. He seems to have thought something had happened that a federal peace officer should know about."

Netty leaned forward and clutched Longarm's arm. "Help her, Marshal. I don't know what has happened with my baby, but find out, please, and help her."

"Then tell me whatever you can about her and her grandparents."

"I have to start getting things ready for the boys to come in from working," she said. "Then after that I will answer any questions that I can."

Chapter 21

After a somewhat late supper Longarm gave his thanks and his good nights to Coon Morgan—the man did indeed have dark rings around his deeply sunken eyes, giving rise to the name—and to his two cowhands, then returned to the table, where Netty was clearing away the last of the dishes.

"It is becoming a little chilly, don't you think?" she said. "Let me finish this and we can go into the cookhouse to talk some more. Then you can bed down in there. Nice as it is during the day, at this time of year the nights can be cold and you wouldn't want to sleep outside unless you had to."

"Is there anything I can do? Bring some wood in or anything?"

"Gracious, what a gentleman." She laughed, then said, "If you're serious, yes. You might bring in an armload of wood. The pile is . . ."

"I see it." Someone, presumably the cowhands, had already split at least two cords of aspen and stacked it on the south side of the cookhouse where come winter it would be out of the prevailing north winds.

He gathered as much as he could handle and carried it

inside the dugout. There was a stone fireplace at the back, but then had there been a stove he was sure Netty would have cooked on that instead of outdoors. The floor had been dug deep, giving the dugout more space and headroom than was apparent from the outside. There was a large open area with no furnishings at all, where they probably moved the table in winter, and a blanket-covered bunk pegged into a side corner.

Longarm dumped his load of wood into a box beside the fireplace and, while he was there, touched a match to the wood that had already been laid ready for lighting. The dry aspen tinder caught quickly, and just as quickly enveloped the larger chunks, until there was a good fire burning. Aspen burns well but does not give out as much heat as pine. On the other hand one tends to burn what one has, and Morgan's outfit had aspen.

Once the fire was well started, he went back out for more wood. By the time Netty joined him, the wood box was full and the fire had filled the dugout with a comforting heat and with the delicate fragrance of the wood smoke.

The woman smiled and motioned Longarm toward the bunk. "Sit down there, Marshal. I'll pull your boots off. Here, let me have your coat too. Make yourself comfortable."

Longarm sat. Netty knelt in front of him and tugged his boots off. Then, surprising him, she started unfastening the buttons of his fly.

"Listen, I, uh . . ."

She looked up at him and smiled. "Do you mind?"

"Do I mind, um, what exactly?"

"Marshal Long, you are a lovely, lovely man. Very strong and handsome." She glanced down toward what her busy fingers were encountering. "Oh, my." Netty laughed again. "A very *big*, handsome man," she said.

"In case you haven't already guessed, Marshal, I am not a shy woman and I simply like sex. I like men. I like men's dicks. I especially like for a man's dick to be inside me. Does that make me a slut? Probably. Certainly it means I am not a respectable woman, but I am not a whore. I get as much as I give and I like what I get. If this bothers you . . . if you don't want to be with a woman who is older than you or if you are being true to someone somewhere, well, just say so. You can go to sleep and I'll not bother you." She smiled. "But I can promise you a fine ride if you don't mind me continuing here." She released the last button and gave his cock a friendly squeeze.

Longarm smiled and said, "Lemme get rid o' this gun-belt and such whilst you shuck yourself outa those clothes"

Before he knew it, Longarm was grabbing hold of both sides of the bunk and hanging on, and Netty was on top of him, bucking and humping for all she was worth. She had promised a fine ride? Well she damn well was delivering one.

There was no way he was going to ask, but judging by the steel gray in her hair she had to be pushing fifty. Very likely pushing it down from above that age would be his guess.

Certainly she was of an age where her tits were drooping toward her belly button and her nipples spread out like a pair of tea saucers pasted to the tips of those dugs.

Her pussy hair was scant and gray and her belly protruded more than a little.

But she was one helluva woman for all of that. Handsome. And lusty.

And Lordy but she could suck a cock. She took it in wet and sloppy, making little gobbling noises all the while she slurped and suckled and damn near drove him wild.

After he came the first time, she kept on sucking until he

again was hard as a cast iron poker, then she duckwalked up to his waist and planted one knee on each side of his hips. Her cunt was slimy with her juices and it gaped wide for his entry.

She lifted herself over him with practiced ease and lowered her hips to skewer herself on his pulsing shaft.

Netty moaned with pleasure as he filled her to capacity, and then she began bucking and thrusting, rotating her hips around and around as well as lifting herself high and slamming down again to punish his belly with the protruding bones of her pelvis.

All Longarm had to do was lie there and hang on to the bunk lest he get bucked off the damn thing.

He was not entirely sure, but he thought it entirely possible that he indeed *would* be bucked off the bed by this wild woman.

Not that he was complaining.

Not likely.

He closed his eyes and lay there, Netty bouncing her ass up and down on him, all the while with a small, happy smile on his face.

Chapter 22

Come morning, Netty gave him a quick blow job and a huge breakfast. She piled cold biscuits and spicy jerky into a clean flour sack for him to carry on the road and said, "I've never been to Baggs, so I can't tell you how to get to the Crowne ranch."

"That's all right. I been t'Baggs before. It ain't so big that I won't be able to find the place." He kissed her. "I'm just sorry I had to be the one to carry the news about your papa's murder."

"Wasn't your doing," Netty said. "But I hope you will be the one to catch the son of a bitch that killed my old daddy."

"I'll do my best. You can count on that," he promised.

From the Morgan place Longarm reined the gray gelding southeast, back to Medicine Bow, rather than heading directly southwest to Baggs. He needed to turn Birdwell's gray in at the livery—and sign a voucher to pay for the mare that had been killed in the line of duty. From there the quickest way down to Baggs would be to hop a westbound train to Rawlins and hire another horse there for the last leg south.

It probably would be easier to take a stagecoach down to Baggs, but in the tiny town there might not be a saddle horse for hire and he purely did hate having to cover new ground in a buggy or a wagon.

Longarm napped on the Union Pacific train—after first making sure the conductor would wake him when they reached Rawlins—and felt considerably refreshed when he stepped down from the passenger coach. He had not gotten much sleep the night before and needed that rest.

"Sure I got horses for the hire, mister," the liveryman told him. "Got good ones, bad ones, and indifferent ones. Which kind would you like?"

Longarm chuckled and said, "You know your animals. You choose one of the good ones for me, please."

The gentleman brought out a rangy dun that had a mean look in its eye. The beast took one look at the bit in the liveryman's hand and pinned its ears flat.

"Here, you son of a bitch," the fellow snarled. He forced the dun's head down and jammed the bit hard against its teeth.

Could be there was a pretty good reason why the horse was cantankerous, Longarm thought. Not that it was any of his business, but there were better ways to treat an animal.

It took something of a tussle, but the stableman managed to get bridle and saddle onto the dun, then handed the reins to Longarm. "All yours, mister. Bring him back when you're done with him."

Longarm more than half suspected that the stableman was wanting to have a little amusement out of this deal. Likely he wanted to enjoy the show while one Custis Long was getting his ass bucked off the horse.

Well, if it was a show he wanted, it was a show he would get.

Longarm vaulted onto the dun's back and clamped his legs tight to the horse's barrel.

By some odd chance the dun's hind end happened to be pointed toward the liveryman at the time. The horse's powerful hindquarters bunched and both back legs lashed out. One hoof caught the livery man square in the stomach, missing his nuts by inches.

The man doubled over and Longarm quickly reined the dun away. After all, he wanted to give the idiot a lesson, not kill him.

Longarm sat the dun through four more powerful explosions of muscle and fury before he guided the horse out into the street, reining it down long enough for him to find the stirrups. Then he eased off the pressure on the horse's mouth and let it blow off some steam.

The horse had both power and spirit, and he suspected the man at the Rawlins livery stable had chosen a horse that was much better than the fellow realized.

"All right, old son," Longarm muttered aloud. "Let's you an' me do some travelin'."

The dun, he noticed, turned its ears about at the sound of his soothing voice. When Longarm nudged it with his heels, the horse flicked its ears forward again and set out at a swift, smooth road gait.

Longarm was smiling when he rode south toward Baggs.

Chapter 23

There just was not a whole hell of a lot to Baggs. A handful of stores surrounded by a scattering of houses and that was it. It was fine country for cows, though, with good grass and some surface water. Not so good for farming, because of the rock lying just beneath the surface of the soil. A few windmills jutting above the skyline suggested there was water not too far underground. All in all, Longarm thought, mighty good country.

The dun stepped high and handsome down the road from Rawlins and gave him no trouble at all along the way. Indeed, Longarm thought, it was a much better horse than its owner knew. The animal just needed an easy hand and some exercise. Likely it was bored just standing inside a small pen day in and day out. Longarm had no business owning a horse, but if he did, he would want one like this.

He pulled up outside a general mercantile that had a UNITED STATES POST OFFICE sign posted in a front window. Other signs indicated the store was also a stagecoach station, a buyer of wool, a dealer in farm equipment, and a telegraph operator, plus proudly proclaiming that the proprietor was one Alvin D. Zaum.

Longarm tied the dun at the hitching rail and entered the cluttered store. A thin man, bald as a boiled egg, was behind the counter. He wore spectacles and an apron so spotlessly white as to almost blind a man from the glare. Well, almost.

"You would be Mr. Zaum, I presume?" Longarm said.

"You presume correctly, sir," the gent in the apron said.

Longarm introduced himself.

"It's a pleasure to meet you, Marshal. How may I help you?" Zaum asked.

"I'm lookin' for a gent name of Carl Crowne or anyways his family. I'm told they have a place somewhere around here."

"Oh, yes. Henry Crowne and Henrietta are fine folks. I've known them for some years now. You won't find any finer."

"Could you tell me how to get to their place, please?"

"Easily done. You ride due east about eight miles then take the track south for another three and there you are. Is there anything else I can do for you?"

Longarm smiled. "Two things. No, make that three. First, I'm lookin' for their granddaughter Justine. D'you know if she's out at the Crowne place?"

"That I cannot tell you. I haven't seen Justine of late, but that doesn't mean anything. She doesn't come to town very often. So what is your second question?"

"Food. Is there anyplace in town where a man could find a meal?" Longarm asked.

"Oh, now that one is easy enough. Right down the block here," he pointed, "is a fine place. There isn't a sign posted, but you can tell where I mean by the blue roller blinds at the windows. Consuela serves excellent food at a modest price."

"Thank you, sir."

"And you said you had three questions?"

Longarm smiled. "Yes, sir. Cigars. Would you happen to have any good cheroots? Something fresh with the tobacco not dried out yet."

Zaum smiled right back, reached beneath his counter, and brought out a large, brown glass thermidor with a cork lid. "I have just the thing for you."

A few minutes later Longarm was back outside, this time with a good supply of excellent cheroots in his pocket and a rumbling in his belly at the thought of food.

He found the blue window blinds Zaum had mentioned and went inside. He was immediately surrounded by the aroma of grease and spices. The place was very nearly full, but Longarm found a stool at one end of the counter and eased down onto it. Henry and Henrietta Crowne could wait another few minutes.

Chapter 24

Half an hour later, with his belly warmed on the inside and a fresh cheroot between his teeth, Longarm walked out onto the main street of Baggs once again.

He found a small barn that sold feed and hay and purchased a gallon of mixed grain for the dun. He tied the sack of grain to his saddle for use later and led the horse to a public trough. Longarm pumped fresh water into the trough while the horse drank, and when it was done, he tightened his cinch and again swung into the saddle.

He reined the dun east.

He was about three miles out when he caught a glimpse of the slanting late afternoon sunlight glinting off polished metal at the base of a large, black gray boulder.

Longarm dropped off the saddle, putting his full weight onto his left stirrup and clinging to the saddle horn with his right hand. Ducked down low like that, he could not be seen by whoever was observing him from two hundred or so yards distant.

It was not that he knew with certainty that the ambusher he'd encountered up at Medicine Bow had followed him down here. But he was damn sure not going to bet his life against it.

"Hiyyup, horse," he clucked. As soon as the dun quickened its pace into a run, Longarm swung back into the saddle. He leaned low against the horse's neck and got the hell away from there.

A few rather cautious hours later Deputy United States Marshal Custis Long found the Crowne homestead.

He was guided to it by a plume of dark smoke.

Of the house there remained only blackened timber and smoldering, still hot embers.

The other buildings on the place, including a small barn and a large chicken house, were unscathed.

Longarm tied the dun well away from the stench of fireblackened timbers, then looked in and around what remained of the place.

There was no sign of Henrietta or of Henry Crowne, although a hint of a scent like that of roasted meat suggested where he could find the couple.

The ashes of the freshly burned house would have to cool before Longarm could confirm his suspicions though.

The same man who'd tried to ambush him had done this? Or an associate?

Longarm scowled at the thought.

His actions, though, were outwardly calm as he unsaddled the dun and put it in a stall in Crowne's otherwise empty barn. He poured the grain into a corner trough in the stall, added a large armload of hay that he found in the loft, and carried a bucket of water from Crowne's well.

Longarm tossed more hay down and piled it into another of the four stalls to make a rudimentary bed for himself. He would not be able to poke through the burned remains of the house until morning at the very least, and he wanted to do that before he decided on his next move.

It was, he thought, a very good thing that he ate before he rode out of Baggs, because it looked like supper and then breakfast to follow would consist of cold water from Crowne's pump.

But what the hell was going on here?

Was this what Mose Arthur had been worried about? Was this what the old man wanted to tell Longarm about back there in Cheyenne?

Longarm had more questions than answers. Or he did right now. He damn sure intended to find those answers and more.

In the meantime he could count on a cold night's sleep and a hungry one.

Chapter 25

Come dawn Longarm again watered the horse and gave it grain from a bin that he found in Crowne's barn. He also carried a peck of the grain into the chicken house, which he had discovered that morning, unscathed, and scattered it for the birds. He left the pen open so the chickens could get out to forage for themselves once he was gone. Otherwise they would surely starve to death. On the other hand, when they escaped their confinement, they would be fodder for hawks and foxes and the other natural predators.

While he was in there, he collected eggs—eleven of them, and it would be hard to find any fresher than these—for his breakfast.

He started a fire using wood from Crowne's woodpile and made a quick foray into the blackened, smoldering remains of the house to fetch a skillet that was still sitting atop Henrietta Crowne's cast iron range, likely the ranch wife's pride and joy.

That stove and a naked chimney were pretty much all that still stood upright. Everying else had literally been "burned to the ground" as the saying went.

He kicked through the mess in the vicinity of the stove and found a serving spoon to go with the skillet.

He also, much to his disgust, found what looked like the bones of a human hand, cracked and discolored by the fire but still recognizable. That would be Henrietta, he guessed. He did not look any further. That could wait until later.

Longarm was possessed of a strong stomach, but he wanted to get some food into that stomach before he got to poking around in search of bodies.

He carried the skillet and large spoon out of the ashes and rinsed them off at the pump. Stuck his boots under the flow of water too to cool them down. There were still active coals in the mess that had been a house and a home, and much of that heat had transferred through the leather of his boot soles.

He had no lard or tallow to put into the skillet, so a scant depth of water would have to do. He set the skillet over his fire and cracked the eggs—every one of them—in. With neither grease nor spatula to make the cooking easier he simply stirred the whole mess around, and once the eggs more or less solidified, he pulled the skillet off the stove.

There was probably some coffee somewhere in what was left of the house, but it was not important enough for another trip into the still hot timbers. He settled for cold water from the pump to go with his scrambled eggs and ate, grateful for a better breakfast than he might have gotten. He might have had to settle for just the cold water for his meal.

When he was done eating, Longarm found a sturdy hoe in a shed attached to the side of the barn. It would be just the thing for the necessary poking and prodding through the ashes. He took a deep breath and steeled his nerve, then ventured back into the ruins of what had been Henry and Henrietta's proud home.

Chapter 26

"Two bodies," Longarm said. "One man, one woman."

Jim Dolan, Baggs's blacksmith and part-time town marshal, shook his head and clucked his tongue. "Henry would be the man, I suppose. The woman could be Henrietta or Justine, either one."

"The grandmother," Longarm said. "Unless the girl had gray hair. I found a few sprigs o' hair stuck underneath the skull where they was more or less protected from the flame. The hairs were silver gray."

Dolan grunted. He was a burly man with a belly like a barrel. "Good people, the Crownes." The big man sighed and repeated, "Good people."

"They hadn't been killed any too long ago," Longarm said, "or anyway they hadn't been burned all that long ago, for the house was still smokin' an' smolderin' when I got there. The ashes was still plenty hot. Call it the day before yesterday that they was killed an' their place burned down."

"Accident, do you think?" Dolan asked.

"Not a chance. The back of the man's head was smashed in an' there was a bullet hole square in the woman's forehead." Longarm paused. "I didn't take time to bury them. Reckon you should send somebody out to take care of that. And there's some chickens running loose. Seems a shame to let them go to feed the hawks. You might tell whoever you send to take a crate or two for them as can be caught."

"I'll do that. Thanks." Dolan pursed his lips, his brow furrowing in thought. Then he shook his head. "There's been no strangers coming through except you. None that didn't get right back on the stage after the rest stop here, that is."

"You keep track?" Longarm asked.

"Of course. It's my job." Dolan looked offended by the question. "I may not be but a small town lawman, but I do what I can."

"There was no second male body. What about the son? Justine's daddy?"

"Carl hasn't been seen around here in two, three years or thereabouts. He's a bad one, Carl is. Did some time up to Laramie a while back. Hasn't been back to see his folks since."

"In the territorial prison, d'you mean?" Longarm asked.

Dolan nodded. "I never did get it straight what Carl did that time. Whatever it was happened outside of the basin." He made that sound like anything taking place outside the immediate vicinity of Baggs might as well have been happening on the surface of the moon, and surely no information could flow so far. Or be of any concern if by some fluke it did.

"And the girl. Justine. Tell me about her, please."

"Sweetest kid you ever seen," Dolan said. "Prettiest too. Big eyes. Always had herself fixed like she was dressed for an Easter parade, even in the middle of the week. But not stuck-up. No, sir, not a bit of it. Any sort of favor you'd need, Justine would be there ready to help. Didn't matter how she was dressed or if it meant getting herself dirty, the girl just wanted to be helpful."

"How old is she?" Longarm asked.

"Oh, twenty, I'd say, give or take a couple years. Carl and his missus wasn't living around here when Justine was born, so I couldn't tell you for sure. If you want to know more about Justine, about the whole Crowne family, or for that matter about anyone around here, you go see Lady Howard."

"Lady?"

Dolan chuckled. "That isn't what it sounds like. We don't have any English royals around here. Lady is her real first name. Howard is her married name. Was a Spencer originally. Now she's widowed, of course."

Longarm did not ask how this Lady person came to be widowed. He really did not give a damn. But he would be pleased if the woman could tell him something about the Crownes and in particular about Justine Crowne. "Where can I find her?"

Dolan beckoned Longarm to follow. He stepped out the back of the smithy, to the small corral where he put horses waiting to be shod. There was a mule standing there now, hipshot and content beside a water trough.

"It isn't far," he said, pointing. "You just go . . ."

Chapter 27

The Howard house was a square, upright two-story affair of the sort that Longarm imagined would be more appropriate in a seaside Massachusetts town than sitting by itself on the outskirts of Baggs, Wyoming. There was ornate gingerbread trim above the porch overhang and even at the eaves of the roofline.

A swing was conveniently placed on the porch where a person could sit and from afar watch the comings and the goings of the town. The yard was enclosed by a white picket fence with roses flourishing inside the tiny space.

Longarm let himself in through the gate and mounted the steps to the porch. He removed his hat and slicked his hair back with a swipe of his hand before he rapped on the screen door.

After a brief delay he heard footsteps approach and a young woman responded. She wore an apron and had a smudge of something white, flour perhaps, on the bridge of her nose. Apart from that, however, she was rather pretty. Longarm guessed her age to be somewhere in her early to mid thirties. She stepped to the door but did not open it. "Yes?" she said.

"Afternoon, miss. I'm lookin' for Miz Howard."

"And you would be . . . ?"

"Deputy United States marshal, miss. Here on official business. Now, are you gonna let me see Miz Howard or not?"

"Official business, you say. Oh, my. Yes, do come in." She unlatched the door and pushed it open for Longarm's entry. "In here, please," she said, guiding him through the foyer to a small parlor. "Have a seat, Deputy. One moment, please."

"Thank you. Now would you please tell Miz Howard that she has a visitor."

The girl gave him an odd look, then turned and disappeared into the rear of the house. Longarm shrugged and chose a seat in a plush armchair upholstered in a shiny blue sateen. The chair looked more comfortable than it felt, but then this was a room decorated to a woman's taste and not for a man's comfort. Longarm thought the now dead Mr. Howard, whoever he may have been, might well have been pleased to escape.

He heard some clatter from the back of the place and then silence for a minute or so, before the maid once again put in an appearance, this time carrying a silver tray with two cups of coffee and a plate of freshly baked scones on it. She first offered Longarm one of the cups then set the tray down on a serving table. While she was in the kitchen, she'd shed the apron and removed the smudge of flour from her nose.

Longarm was taken somewhat aback when the serving girl settled onto a chair with a cup and a scone. She tucked her feet up underneath her and took a sip of the coffee. "Now, what is this official business of yours, Deputy?"

"You, uh, you are Mrs. Howard."

She giggled. "I am," she said. "Lady Spencer Howard." It was obvious that having been mistaken for a maidservant amused her. Damn good thing it did too, Longarm thought. Lady Howard could well have been pissed off by his erroneous assumptions.

"I'm sorry, Miz Howard," he said, standing and half bowing toward her before resuming his seat. In the process he slopped some coffee into his saucer, so he carefully poured it back into the cup, shrugged, and took a sip. The brew was hot and stout and tasty. "Reckon I should introduce myself. I'm Deputy Custis Long, ridin' out of the Denver office. I'm here 'cause I'm told you are a woman as knows the folks around here."

Lady Howard laughed. It was a hearty sound without reserve. When she laughed, her nose wrinkled and crow's-feet appeared at the corners of her eyes. Which were, he noticed now, bright blue. "You mean because I am the town busybody, is that it?"

"Oh, I don't know as I woulda put it exactly that way," he said, "but, well, yes."

"Fair enough, Mr. Long. What is it that you need to know?"

He explained but not in detail. He had no desire to shock the pretty widow.

"And you want to know about Henry and Henrietta, is that it?"

"Actually it's their granddaughter Justine I wanna ask about. She seems to be missing, and I can't help but wonder if the murders of her grandparents . . . her other grandfather, Moses Arthur, was also murdered recently, that was over in Cheyenne . . . I can't help but wonder if her disappearance isn't somehow connected with those killings. So anything you might could tell me about Justine just might be a help to me."

"Then I think you have come to the right place, Deputy. I know Justine fairly well. But can I ask you, do you have plans for dinner? We could talk about Justine over a roast chicken that I happen to have in the oven and really need to tend to before it dries out."

"That's nice of you, ma'am, if it'd be no bother."

"Bother? It would be a pleasure. I so seldom have company when I dine. It will be nice to have someone to talk with over dessert."

Chapter 28

"Is this the, um, dessert?" Longarm murmured.

Lady giggled agreement that indeed it was, arching her back and guiding his head across the flat of her belly to the nest of curly blond pubic hair below.

Longarm's tongue probed, found the smooth, wet valley of her slit, then began to flicker back and forth across the tiny bump of her clitoris.

Lady responded with wild gyrations of her hips, thrusting herself harder onto his lips and trying to stifle a sound that came out somewhere between a squeal and a scream.

Longarm lifted his head out of her crotch, his mustache tickling her pussy as he did so, and laughed. "You do come mighty easy, don't you, girl."

"Are you complaining, sir?"

"I am not."

"Then why don't you go back to what you were doing, because, darling man, I am just getting warmed up."

Longarm smiled. And did as the lady bid.

The supper they'd shared late that afternoon had been light and not all that good. But Lady's charms were more than enough to improve the meal, and it turned out that she was as direct as she was pretty.

At the end of the meal, she gave him a long, calm look then casually asked, "Do you like to fuck?"

"More than passing well," he said as he struggled to hide his surprise.

"So do I," Lady told him, "but I have to be careful what my neighbors think." She laughed. "They like to gossip almost as much as I do."

"There's times," he said, "when bein' a stranger in town has its advantages. After all, who would I tell about things? Leastways not till I get back to Denver."

"My point exactly," Lady declared. "And you are an uncommonly handsome man."

Longarm laughed. "Handsome? Not hardly."

"Virile, then? Will you grant me 'virile'?"

"If you think so, sure."

"Exciting certainly. And you say you like to fuck. Are you good at it?"

"Lordy," he said, "I can't recall ever bein' asked that before. I'm not real sure how to answer it."

"Well if you can't *tell* me, perhaps you can *show* me," Lady declared.

Longarm chuckled. "Reckon we can talk business later." He reached for her. Lady stood and came willingly into his arms.

She was taller than he had realized and thin, but once she got her clothes off—which she did in very short order—she proved to be attractively slender, with firm breasts and pale nipples.

She took him by the hand and led him to her bedroom, which was small and tidy and smelled of a delicate perfume, the same scent he discovered on her body as soon as they were horizontal.

Longarm buried his face between her breasts and was content for a moment to simply breathe in Lady's delicious scent. But there was more to her than that. Much, much more.

She started to take the lead, but he took her by the arm and pulled her back, making it clear that he would be in charge.

Lady acquiesced willingly, giving herself to him readily, her taut body practically vibrating with pent-up desire as she licked his nipples and fondled his balls before working her way down to his cock and taking it deep into her mouth.

"I want you to come in my mouth the first time," Lady told him. "It will take the edge off so you have more staying power after that." She giggled. "Besides, I like it. I like the feel of it and the taste of it and just about everything there is between a man and a woman."

"You can take it in your mouth for a spell," he consented, "but when I get to wanting the feel of your pussy, I'll put it there or wherever I damn well please."

"Yes, sir. Whatever you say."

And so it had been, Lady compliant to his wishes and quick to climax, coming time and time again to the touch of his hands, his tongue, and to the pounding of his cock driving deep inside her.

The two of them lay locked on her bed until well after dark. Finally Longarm rolled off of her and sat up on the edge of the bed while Lady found matches and lighted a bedside lamp.

"D'you still have some o' that good coffee?" he asked.

"It probably tastes old by now."

"I don't care. Pour me some."

"Yes, of course."

"Then we can talk a little about Justine Crowne."

"There isn't much I can tell you about her," Lady said.

"She became involved with a gambler," she shuddered, "a genuinely evil man. I know she was head over heels for him. She trusted me, you should understand. She came to me several times to talk about things she couldn't take to her grandparents."

"I can understand that sorta thing," Longarm said.

"Of course. I advised her against Edgar."

"Who is this Edgar?"

"Like I said, a gambler. A local man, Edgar Spurlock. Justine was crazy about him. I know for a fact that she gave her virginity to him, because we talked about that both before she did it and again afterward. I know she intended to be with him. Marriage, I mean. The son of a bitch is the kind to use a girl then dump her, although she wouldn't believe me when I told her that. I know he was with her one afternoon. That was in a shack down close to the hog ranch where he works a card table. Then she disappeared. She simply disappeared. I never heard from her again, even though she promised faithfully that she would write to me from wherever they went. As it turned out, though, Justine left but that bastard Edgar did not. He still deals poker at a place south of town, across the line into Colorado, so our law has no say over him."

"But Justine told you she would be with this Spurlock?"

Lady nodded and playfully licked Longarm's shoulder.

"Careful or you'll get me started again," Longarm warned her.

Lady's answer was an impish grin and another lick. "What about that coffee you wanted?"

Longarm pushed her flat onto the bed. "The coffee can wait, woman. Now lay quiet an' open them legs to me."

Which she willingly did.

Chapter 29

It would have been easier to take the stagecoach south, particularly so since he had gotten practically no sleep the night he spent with Lady, but he wanted the freedom of movement that a saddle horse gave him, so he kept the dun horse he'd hired in Rawlins.

There was no need for directions to the hog ranch where Edgar Spurlock was a house dealer. Any place like that would thrive on trade passing by and so would have to be located on or very close to the public road that ran from Baggs down to Craig, Colorado, and beyond. All Longarm had to do was point the dun south and look for the surveyor's monument that marked the dividing line between Wyoming Territory and the state of Colorado.

He would find the slop joint not too far south of that line. Likely he would find Spurlock there. And—he hadn't wanted to tell Lady Howard what he expected—he'd probably find Justine Crowne there as well.

When a man like Spurlock courted an exceptionally pretty girl like Justine was said to be, there usually was more than one reason, and getting a piece of ass was normally the least of it. Turning her out as a whore was probably the rest of that equation. Longarm fully expected to find Justine turning tricks in some shack adjacent to the saloon, close to Baggs but too ashamed of her fall from decency to come home again.

Longarm pondered his theory while the dun traveled on a slack rein.

There was a fly in that ointment, he realized.

If that was all there was to this, why had Moses Arthur claimed to have a problem that would involve federal laws being broken. Prostitution was against no federal law that Longarm knew of. Neither was murder.

Of course there was no way for him to know at this late date just how much Mose Arthur knew of the law. It could well be that the old man knew his granddaughter was hooking in Colorado and so could not be reached by Wyoming law. Maybe that was why he wanted a deputy United States marshal to tackle the matter.

Even assuming that, Longarm thought . . . so what.

He hooked a leg over the saddle horn and let the dun continue on. Longarm pulled a cheroot from his coat—he was beginning to run low on them and needed to buy more as soon as the opportunity arose—and bit the twist off, then carefully licked the tightly rolled wrapper leaf and lighted his smoke.

He did not know what it was, but there was something satisfying about a good cigar. Smoking one seemed to help him to think.

A second fly appeared in his mental ointment as he pondered what little he knew about Justine Crowne and Moses Arthur. If this was only a simple matter of crossing jurisdictions—*when no laws seemed to have been broken anyway*—why were Arthur and the Crownes murdered? And why did someone take a shot at him up near Medicine Bow?

What it came down to, he had to admit, was that there was a hell of a lot at play here that he did not at this point suspect.

Whatever it was justified murder in someone's mind. Three murders that he knew about and possibly more that he did not.

Longarm heard the thunder of hooves and the rattle of trace chains coming up behind. He dropped his leg and found the stirrup again, then reined the dun off the road to make way for the southbound stagecoach.

The driver waved a friendly hello as the light mud wagon clattered past with two passengers on the benches, both of them with handkerchiefs held to their noses to keep the thickly billowing dust out. Neither of the passengers waved, but Longarm could not be sure either of them saw him there beside the road.

"I see what looks to be a creek over there, old son," Longarm said to the horse, getting a flick of its ears in response. "Let's go see if you're thirsty. Then I'm gonna take me a little nap before we trot on down to that hog ranch an' see what we can see. It might could be that I should have my wits about me when we get there."

Chapter 30

Longarm had spotted the hog ranch a little past noon. It lay a hundred yards or so east of the road, tucked up against a massive rock face. A spacious corral was built on the north side of the saloon, while on the south there was a long, low line of cribs for the whores. From the road he could see two of the soiled doves sitting in the doorways of their cribs waiting for customers.

The place seemed to be popular enough. There were half a dozen horses already standing idle in the corral. Longarm added the dun to that collection.

A well had been drilled between the saloon and the corral. He stopped there to pump some of the cold, clean water. He drank a little first, then splashed his face and neck to rinse off some of the dust of the road. He felt refreshed after he did so.

Longarm slicked his hair back with one hand, wiped his face with his handkerchief, and replaced his hat. He squared his shoulders and headed for the door leading into the saloon.

The place was bigger than it had appeared from the outside. A lack of windows was made up for by the numerous lamps placed on the walls and hanging from the ceiling. But then windows to bring in daylight were not important to a business that would be conducted mostly at night.

A long bar lay on the left or north side of the big room. Tables for drinking—or gambling—were ranked along the south wall. The middle of the place was open, an expanse of plank floor where patrons could dance. At the back there was a foot-high platform with a few chairs on it. That would be for a small band, Longarm assumed, although there were no musicians present at this early hour. Likely they would appear sometime past sundown and play as long as there were customers to keep the money flowing.

At the moment there were two men standing at the bar and four more gathered around a card table, one of them a dude with a yellow brocade vest, string tie, and hair so loaded with oil that it gleamed in the lamplight. That one, he suspected, would be Edgar Spurlock. Longarm ignored Spurlock and approached the bar instead.

Longarm tipped his Stetson back from his forehead and smiled. "Howdy," he said to the man behind the bar, who was wearing an apron, a spotlessly clean apron, he noticed. "Would it be possible for a gent to get a bite to eat here?"

The bartender came down to Longarm's end of the bar and said, "Friend, you can get most anything a man needs. You say it's food that you're wanting?"

"Food an' prob'ly a little more. I've about rode far enough for one day." He laughed. "My butt ain't used to this abuse, an' my legs is about to fold up underneath me if I don't light an' rest for a spell."

"We have a good kitchen out back," the barman said. "You can get a full dinner for seventy five cents or a bowl of stew and slab of cornbread for a quarter. Either one comes with a beer included."

Longarm nodded. "I'll have the stew an' I'll take that beer now if you don't mind."

The bartender drew the beer and set it in front of Longarm, then stepped out of sight into a back room for a moment. When he returned, he said, "Your lunch will be right out. Help yourself to a seat and it will be brought to you."

"Thanks," Longarm said, lifting his beak from the foamy suds on his beer. He smacked his lips and said, "This is good." He saluted the bartender with his upraised mug, then turned and chose a table close to the card players, close enough that he could listen in on their conversation.

The barman must have passed word that there was a fresh fish in the place, for a girl soon appeared in the doorway. She was very young, the freshness of youth buried beneath a thick layer of powder and rouge. She wore a bright yellow dress that fell only to her knees. The bodice was tight and cut low enough to show what little cleavage she had. That was not very much actually, as her tits were little more than bumps under the cloth. Her pale blond hair was pulled back in a severe bun. She had freckles, he noticed. And a bruise on the left side of her face that the makeup could not completely hide.

The girl came swaying over to the table where Longarm sat. "Hi, honey. Do you want company?" Without waiting for an answer, she pulled a chair close beside Longarm's and dropped onto it. "My name is Honey, honey. What's yours?" She smiled and placed her hand on his forearm.

"John," Longarm said.

"I'm happy to meet you, John. Buy me a drink? I would like that." She squeezed his arm ever so lightly.

"Sure," he said. "What would you like?"

"I'm real partial to champagne, John. Would that be all right?"

"Sure thing, Honey."

The girl waved to the barman, who very quickly brought a dark green bottle of the bubbly along with a pair of glasses. The pop of the cork when he opened it suggested that it was genuine champagne.

"Would you like another beer or will you settle for the wine?" the bartender asked.

"I'll stick with the beer," Longarm said.

Immediately after the champagne arrived so did his stew and a plate of corn dodgers and a small tub of sweet butter, carried out on a tray borne by a short, stout, swarthy woman. Mexican, Longarm thought, or Indian.

"Are you hungry, Honey?" he asked.

She shook her head and poured herself a foaming glass of the champagne. She quickly drained the first glass and poured another. Steeling herself with spirits, he figured. Preparing for a chore she would rather not do?

She drank that one down too and poured a third glass.

While Honey was busy with her fancy wine, Longarm dug into the stew. He did not know what the meat was, but the stew was good, thick with potatoes and carrots and swimming in rich gravy. The corn dodgers were excellent also, light and sweet. He slathered the butter on good and thick and thoroughly enjoyed his meal.

The barman replaced the beer mugs, a fresh one arriving as soon as one was emptied. Probably Honey was giving the bartender signals, but Longarm did not notice how.

The girl had worked her way through most of the bottle of champagne by the time Longarm was done eating.

She took his arm and leaned her head against his shoulder. She smelled of lilac water and sweat. She lifted her face to him and smiled sweetly. "Would you like to go to my room, John? I can make a man *very* happy."

Her hand was on his leg, creeping ever higher toward the bulge that appeared in his britches.

She put her hand on his cock and lightly squeezed. "Very happy," she repeated.

"Let's go," he said, pushing back from the table and rising to his feet.

Chapter 31

Honey's crib was the third door from the road end of the line. The door was secured only by a small block of wood rotating on a single nail. It would keep the door from blowing open in a breeze but would not bar anyone from coming in if they really wanted to. Likely that was deliberate, Longarm thought, in case the management—whoever the hell that might be—had to come to the rescue of one of the whores.

The crib was small, probably six feet across by eight feet deep. The entire back end was a platform the size of the double-wide mattress that lay on it. Underneath the platform was a long drawer, probably where Honey kept her clothing. The bottom third of the mattress was covered with oilcloth. That would be for the "gentlemen" who did not bother to remove their boots. The other two thirds were covered with a threadbare trade blanket. A scrawny pillow was propped against the wall at that end.

The rest of the furnishings consisted of a three-legged stool and half a dozen coat hooks screwed into the left-hand wall. A lamp was mounted on the right-hand wall.

Honey left the door open to admit some light while she struck a match and lighted the lamp, then she pushed the door shut and turned the wooden latch to hold it closed.

She stepped close to Longarm and began unbuttoning his shirt.

The girl presented a problem for him. He did not really want to fuck her. She looked just too damned young, and deputy United States marshals were not supposed to involve themselves in that sort of thing.

On the other hand he did not think it a very good idea for him to announce himself. Not just yet. Not if he wanted to learn more about Justine Crowne and why her entire family was murdered.

It seemed now he either had to admit to being a deputy or climb onto that platform with the more than willing little whore.

Longarm settled for a smile. And a kiss.

The girl tasted of champagne and peanuts. At least that is what he *hoped* he was tasting in her mouth.

He shrugged out of his coat and hung it on a wall hook and then did the same with his gunbelt. By then Honey had his shirt and vest open. She removed his Ingersoll from the watch pocket and stuffed it into the pocket on the other side of the vest, so the watch chain would not interfere; then she pushed both his vest and his shirt off his shoulders.

Longarm opened the buttons on his trousers and sat on the side of the bed while Honey knelt and pulled off his boots before she tugged his pants down.

While Longarm got out of his own balbriggans, Honey very quickly shed her dress. That took only seconds. But then she would have had quite a lot of practice at getting in and out of her clothing.

Her body was slender to the point of being skinny, if a little wide in the hips. Her legs were toothpick thin. Her tits were barely large enough to be considered tits. Her nipples, however, were dark and prominent and rubbery. Her pubic hair was a mass of blond curls. Which answered the question of whether or not she was a natural blond. All in all she was not a bad-looking girl and would have been almost pretty without all that makeup.

She still looked awfully damned young though. She removed whatever it was that had been holding her hair back and, with a shake of her head, let a tawny mane fall loose. She did not look quite so young when she did that.

"You lie down, honey," she said, "and let me give you some pleasure."

Longarm stretched out on his back while Honey straddled him, her knees on either side of his hips. She leaned forward and began to lick his nipples, the sensation shooting all the way down into his dick, which by then was standing at rigid attention.

"D'you mind if I ask you something, Honey?" he asked.

The girl looked up and frowned, "You aren't going to ask me how a nice girl like me got into a business like this, are you?" He got the impression she had heard that too many times already and did not like it.

"Uh, no," he said. "What I'm wantin' to know is if your real name might be Justine. A fella I know told me to look for a girl name of Justine if I ever got down this way." He smiled and touched her cheek. "If that gives offense, well, I'm sorry. I'm just curious, that's all."

"Oh. Sorry, honey. I've just . . ." She shook her head. "Never mind. Anyway, about your question, no, my name isn't Justine and I don't know anyone here whose name is. There was a girl by that name that came here a few weeks ago, but she isn't one of us girls. She was just passing through. All right? Can we get back to business now?"

Business. The word sort of took the edge off things.

Still, Honey wasn't a bad-looking girl and Longarm's interest revived when she bent to run her tongue up and down his cock.

She sucked on him until he was hard as a tent pole again, then mounted him, her fingers toying with his nipples while her hips rose and fell, rotating at the same time.

Honey was right. She did know how to please a man.

Chapter 32

Longarm stamped his feet to help settle his boots comfortably in place, then took his Stetson down from the wall hook where it had been for the past hour or so. He put the hat on and nudged it in place where he liked it, then touched the grip of his .45 with two fingers to make sure the revolver was exactly where it should be.

"You're a doll," he told Honey as he reached into his pocket.

"Oh, you don't pay me, honey," the girl said. "You should pay Buster out front. He's the one behind the bar. Settle up with him."

"Would it be all right if I give you a tip?" he asked.

Honey grinned. "I guess that would be all right, honey."

Longarm pulled out a silver dollar and placed it on the pillow. Honey squealed with joy and immediately snatched up the dollar and knelt to tug the big, underbed drawer open so she could stash the coin away in a coffee can she kept there. It looked like she had a fair amount saved up. Longarm could not help but wonder what the girl was saving up for, what sort of hope was in her heart.

"Thank you, honey," she said once the dollar was safely put away and the drawer back under the bed.

"My pleasure, Honey," he told her. He meant it too. She was a cheerful little thing and really did please. He touched the brim of his hat to her and let himself out of the crib, making his way back into the saloon.

"Everything all right, friend?" the barman named Buster asked when Longarm ordered another beer.

"Just fine, thanks."

"You want to settle up now or run a tab?" Buster asked.

"How much do I owe you?"

"Let me see now. There's your lunch. Couple extra beers. Bottle of champagne . . . you and Honey didn't finish that, so I put the rest of it away for you whenever you want it, but you'd best drink it soon or it'll go flat . . . and then there's a quickie with Honey. That would come to, oh . . . ," he paused for a moment in thought while he added up the services in his head, "four dollars and forty-five cents."

Longarm placed a pair of bright gold two-dollar-and-fifty-cent quarter eagles on the bar. Buster took them and returned Longarm's change.

Edgar Spurlock was still dealing cards at his table. The same four players were still there. Longarm picked up his beer mug and wandered over in that direction.

"Is there room at the table for one more?" Longarm asked.

Spurlock nodded, pointed with his chin, and said, "Drag that chair over, mister. Bob, Jimmy, you two shift aside a little to accommodate the gentleman." Spurlock looked up, his hands busy shuffling the cards. "If you'd care to give your name, mister . . . ?"

"John," Longarm said. "Call me John."

"I'm Edgar. Eddie if you prefer. Sit down, John, and welcome. The game is stud poker. Open on anything you have." He smiled. "Or want us to think you have. Bet on each card as she comes out. Fifty cent ante and a two-dollar limit on each bet."

Longarm pulled out a cheroot and lighted it, then leaned forward and paid attention to the cards that Eddie was expertly dealing.

Chapter 33

Three hours later Longarm was down about two dollars and a half, but as far as he could tell—and he was very good at spotting card cheats—Edgar Spurlock dealt a clean card game. The gambler was good at his profession, but that was because he played the odds remarkably well, not because of bottom dealing or card substitution.

Spurlock gathered the cards from the table, pulled them together, and passed the deck to a man named Adam, who sat at Spurlock's left.

"I'm going to take a break now," Spurlock announced. "I have to visit the privy and have something to eat, but I'll be back in, oh, an hour or so." He pushed his chair back and stood.

"Deal me out too," Longarm said as he gathered his money and dropped the coins into his coat pocket. He lighted a cheroot and fiddled with his collar for a moment before he stood and stretched, giving him time to see which way Edgar Spurlock went when he left the table.

Longarm suppressed a smile when he saw that Spurlock

headed outside, toward the privy. That, he thought, was perfect.

Striding purposefully out the door as if he too wanted to take a piss, he followed the gambler and watched as the man entered one of the two privies placed there for the use of the saloon patrons.

Longarm wandered over there and looked carefully about to make sure no one was watching.

It was getting on toward evening, and the whores from the nearby cribs were gathered inside having dinner since the evening crowd had not yet arrived. A stagecoach was due in within half an hour, he understood, and there would be a good many more customers around then, so this was probably the best opportunity he would have for what he wanted to do.

He leaned against the side wall of the one-hole privy and waited for Edgar Spurlock to finish whatever he was doing in there. After a minute or two the privy door swung open and Spurlock stepped out.

The man's concentration was on the buttons of his trousers. He looked up when Longarm stepped in front of him. The tall deputy stood nose to nose with Spurlock, put a hand on the man's chest, and pushed, sending him reeling backward inside the tiny outhouse.

"What . . . ? Is this a robbery? Damn you, I played fair with you. You know . . ."

"It ain't a robbery," Longarm snarled, shoving the man again.

The backs of Spurlock's knees hit the bench seat of the privy and he involuntarily sat. Abruptly and probably not very comfortably.

"I didn't . . ."

"Shut the fuck up an' listen to me," Longarm said, towering over the now very nervous gambler. "I am gonna ask you a simple question. I expect a simple answer. If you don't answer me straight or if you lie to me," Longarm said, "what I figure to do is to turn you upside down an' drop you headfirst into the cess pit underneath this here privy. Now." Longarm paused for a breath. "Do you understand me?"

"What is this . . . ?"

"No questions, asshole. Do you understand me? Yes or no?"

"Uh, yes." Spurlock looked extremely uncomfortable. Sweat beaded his forehead, and he seemed pale even in the dim light that penetrated the privy.

"You've probably got a hideout gun somewhere on you," Longarm said. "I wouldn't advise you to go for it, 'cause that would force me to break your arms before I drop you into the shit. You say you understand me? Is that right?"

"Yes, uh, sir."

"Fine. You're doin' fine, Eddie. Now here's your question. Justine Crowne. Where is she?"

Edgar Spurlock looked like he might very well pass out before he could give Longarm an answer to that question. He fingered his tight collar and his mouth gaped like a trout's out of water.

"I can't . . . I mustn't . . ."

"Eddie, I tried to do this the easy way."

Longarm took hold of the hand at Spurlock's collar. The gambler did not even resist.

Taking Spurlock's hand in both of his, Longarm got a firm grip on the man's little finger and with a twist of his wrists broke it at the knuckle.

Spurlock screamed.

Longarm continued to hold the man's hand while he asked again. "Justine Crowne, Eddie. Where is she?"

"I can't, mister. I can't tell. They . . . they'll kill me if I do."

"Suit yourself then." Longarm wrestled Spurlock to his feet and turned him to face the none too clean seat of the privy. The stink of the pit of turds swimming in cold piss underneath the seat rose around them. Spurlock was so terrified he was limp and unable to resist.

He was a handsome son of a bitch, it seemed, but he had no guts. But then, Longarm thought, the sort of man who preys on women would not likely be courageous.

Longarm took hold of the back of Spurlock's trousers and lifted him bodily off his feet, pushing his head down toward the gaping hole beneath which lay the pit full of excrement.

"Please," Spurlock whined.

"Last chance," Longarm told him with another push on the back of Spurlock's head.

Chapter 34

Longarm reined the dun off the road. It was coming evening, and he wanted enough daylight left so he could gather wood for a fire. He found a small bench on a sloping hillside where his camp would be protected from the winds that came sweeping across the empty badlands west of Craig.

A stand of aspen provided the wood, but the only available water was what he carried in the canteen on his saddle.

"Reckon we'll have to rough it this evening, old son," he told the horse. He picketed the dun and removed its bridle, then wet his handkerchief and swabbed out the horse's mouth before pulling a feed bag over its ears.

He had purchased that equipment and a gallon of clean oats back in Craig. The grain was nearly gone now and so was the water. Come morning, it would be nice to find a place where he could buy more grain, but it would be critical that he find a source of water. Both he and the dun needed it.

As it was, once the grain had been eaten, he poured a pint or so of the precious fluid into the leather bottom of the feed bag and let the horse have that to drink. He himself could go without his coffee tonight. He would have to make do with just the strips of jerky and a bite or two of the vile-tasting but energy-rich pemmican he had bought in Craig.

Visions of the fine meals to be had in Quartermane's Chop House in Denver taunted him as he chewed on what passed for a meal in his rudimentary camp.

When he was finished eating, he spread his bedroll—also aquired in the helpful shops in Craig—and kicked the fire apart. He'd barely had time to begin to drowse when he heard the sound of a horse on the road below.

The soft hoofbeats ceased and he heard the low whinny of one horse, answered by that of another. The traveler's horse calling to his dun, or perhaps the other way around. Moments later he heard the rattle of harness and bit chains and the creak of leather.

In the gloom below he could dimly see the outline of a buggy pulled off the side of the road.

"Hello the camp," a voice called up the hillside.

Longarm sat up, his hand not far from the Colt at his side, and answered, "Up here."

"Mind if I join you?"

"Come ahead if you're friendly."

"Aye, that I am."

"Then come an' welcome, though I don't have much left to share tonight. I'm near about outa water."

"That's all right," the voice called again, the source of it coming nearer as the man climbed huffing and puffing toward the bench. "I have water to share. Biscuits and bacon too if you're hungry."

The visitor emerged in the darkness, a fat man wearing a bowler hat and no visible firearms, although Longarm did not intend to put much faith in that observation. Longarm stood to greet the man.

"Felix Batterslea," the man said, extending his hand.

Longarm shook and said, "John Church. How d'you do."

Batterslea smiled and said, "Tired, that's how I am, Mr. Church. I was going to go on a little way more tonight, but I heard your horse and smelled the smoke from your fire. I brought some water. If you're interested, we can use that wood of yours to build up the fire and boil some coffee."

"You have coffee?" Longarm grinned. "Felix, you just became my new best friend."

Batterslea put some coffee on the fire. "What brings you out here, John?"

Longarm shrugged. "Drifting. You?"

"I'm a salesman, John. I deal in fine spirits and gourmet foodstuffs."

"Gourmet, what the hell does that mean, Felix?"

"Fancy, John. It just means fancy."

"So what are you doing way out here in the badlands?"

"Oh, I have an account west of here. A very good account, in fact. I visit there twice a year, all the way from Boston. You wouldn't think it, but the trips are worth my while. I sell brandies, tinned oysters and lobster tails, French wines, things like that. I just came from there. Now I'm on my way back home with a very handsome order in my book." He patted his breast pocket and laughed. "You wouldn't be interested in a purchase, would you?"

"I think maybe not, Felix, but who the devil out here would be in the market for such?"

"Just one customer, actually. A very wealthy eccentric. A state legislator, as it happens. Very powerful as well as wealthy. I won't mention the name, of course, but I am sure you would recognize it if I told you."

"Oh, I reckon you don't have to say it. I know who you'll be meaning."

"I'm sure you do," Batterslea agreed.

"I'm a poor man myself," Longarm said, "but I've always been interested in the ways of the rich. Not mentioning any names, o' course, but tell me all about this fella, would you? Him an' where he lives an' so on?"

Batterslea laughed again. "Now, if there is one thing I am capable of, John, it is talk. Why, I could sit here and talk all night with not much encouragement. Say, I think that coffee is just about ready. Let's have a cup and I will tell you anything you want to know. Probably more than you really want to know, so just tell me when you've heard enough. Or ask whatever you like if you want to hear more."

"Felix, I've got to say, I am mighty glad you stopped here tonight. I'm, uh, pleased for the company." Longarm pushed another handful of aspen pieces onto the fire, wrapped his kerchief around his hand to protect it from the heat, and picked up Felix Batterslea's coffeepot ready to pour into the enamelware cups the fat salesman also provided.

"If it wouldn't offend you, John, I have a little brandy we could use to sweeten that coffee."

"Have I mentioned that you are my new best friend, Felix?" Longarm said with a grin as he poured their coffee. But not too full. He had to leave room for the brandy, after all.

The two rocked back on their heels, and true to his word, Batterslea began to speak. He did not quiet down again for more than an hour.

The man proved to be almost—almost, that is—as informative as Edgar Spurlock had been.

Chapter 35

"Well I'll be a son of a bitch," Longarm muttered aloud.

The dun's right ear swiveled around in response, and the horse tossed its head.

Longarm had thought Felix Batterslea was gilding the lily more than a little, embellishing the truth in order to make his yarns more interesting. If anything, it seemed, the fat man had been holding back in an effort to make himself more believable.

There, an hour's ride ahead and crowning one of the many flat-topped benches to be found in this brown and arid land, was what looked almost exactly like a drawing Longarm had once seen. An illustration in a book about King Arthur or some such. It was a castle. A fucking castle. Out here in the middle of nowhere.

"In-fucking-credible," he said, causing the horse's ear to rotate again toward the sound.

Longarm touched his heel to the dun's flank, and the horse obediently resumed its progress toward the castle.

As he came nearer, Longarm could see that this castle was made of adobe brick, but the high walls and battlements were faithfully rendered as if taken from that same illustration. There was even the top of a square tower visible within the walls. He halfway expected to see archers in scarlet livery standing atop the walls.

There were no archers, but a flag of some sort hung limp from a pole extending from the top of the tower. Longarm could not see whose flag it might be, but it was not the stars and stripes of the United States of America. A personal coat of arms? Perhaps.

As he came near, a puff of breeze from the west filled the flag. It was a lion rampant on a field of white.

That made sense actually, as the flag was flying over the home of State Senator Henry Leon Lyon, the very man Longarm had come here to see.

The well-traveled road climbed to the top of the bench where Lyon's castle lay, and from that level Longarm could see that the castle walls were surrounded by a moat, or what was intended to represent a moat, he supposed. This desert moat was dry but deep.

Dry tumbleweed, rusting tin cans, and scraps of this and that littered the floor of the moat, rendering the effect more of a trash heap than a protection against assault, which was what he assumed the purpose of a moat to be.

A bridge made of heavy timbers crossed the moat to an open gate. Longarm guided the dun across the bridge. The horse was nervous about stepping onto it. The animal balked and tried to turn away, but then gave in to Longarm's insistence.

The horse's hoofbeats rang hollow on the planks underfoot.

Longarm passed beneath the spiked iron gate and rode through a short tunnel into a courtyard that was flanked on two sides by low adobe buildings, two of which had smoke coming from their chimneys. The castle tower was directly ahead. He guessed that building to be thirty or more feet tall, with the square tower top rising even higher.

"Hello," he called, drawing the dun to a halt. "Is anybody here? Hello?"

The response was not exactly what he would have preferred.

Behind him there was a loud clang of iron striking stone. The dun spooked, and for a moment it was all Longarm could do to get the horse calmed and back under control. When he did, he twisted in the saddle to get a look at what caused the noise.

It was the gate, he saw.

Some unseen someone had dropped the damn gate.

Longarm was trapped inside Henry Lyon's castle until or unless Lyon's men raised that gate again.

Chapter 36

A man emerged from a small room just to the right of the
tunnel entry. The fellow was not wearing livery, but he had
the next best thing: He was wearing a badge. He had a hol-
stered revolver on his hip and carried a short-barreled shotgun across his arm.

Longarm swung the dun around to face him and touched
the brim of his Stetson. "Afternoon," he said politely.

"I see you're wearing a sidearm," the badge-toter said.

"Yes, sir. Is there somethin' wrong with that?"

"Inside these walls there is, yes. Take that gunbelt off
and drop it to the ground."

"Pardon me?"

"Do it. Do it now. I have three rifles trained on you." He
nodded toward the wall, where suddenly three men had
indeed materialized. And the three did indeed have rifles
aimed down at Longarm.

"Happy t'oblige," Longarm drawled. He carefully un-
buckled his gunbelt, held it out to the side, and let it drop to
the hard-packed earth underfoot.

The guard—Longarm could not think of any properly

chartered town or township out here that could authorize the lawful issuance of a badge—smiled. "Fine. Now ride away a few steps while I pick that shooter up, please."

Longarm did as he was asked, and the guard moved in behind him to retrieve Longarm's Colt and gunbelt.

"All right. State your business here in Camelot."

"Camelot?" Longarm asked. "Wasn't that . . . ?"

"Never mind the history lesson. Just tell me what you're doing here," the guard demanded, his tone and demeanor suggesting the man was becoming impatient.

Longarm did purely hate the thought of irritating anyone who was holding a shotgun on him. All the more so when Longarm himself happened to be unarmed. "I'm passin' through," he said. "I saw this place. Reckoned I could find water here and maybe something to eat. This horse and I been on short rations for both since sometime yesterday."

The guard nodded. "Fair enough. You can have your fill of food and water and spend tonight. Are you looking for work?"

"Well I ain't looking for a career, but I might could use a few days' pay. Enough to buy some supplies with, say."

The guard grunted. "Tell you what then. I'll take you over to the cookhouse for something to eat, then introduce you to the boss. Any hiring would be up to him, but we always need guards in the mines."

"That sounds good to me," Longarm said, wondering at the same time just what mines the man could be talking about. He did not know of any. Which did not mean there could not be mines here, but it was a curious thing anyway.

"You can tie your horse over there. Follow me and I'll show you where we eat."

"Thanks." Longarm stepped down off the dun and led it to a hitching post at the corner of one of the low-roofed adobe buildings. The guard had not bothered to introduce himself. Nor, come to think of it, had he asked for Long-arm's name.

"This way." The guard led him to another of the buildings, one of those with smoke issuing from a short chimney, and motioned Longarm inside.

The vigas, or ceiling timbers, were not yet gray with age, Longarm noticed. The poles, lodgepole pine he supposed, looked almost freshly peeled, suggesting that these buildings had not been here terribly long. A few years at best.

Inside the long room there was a table flanked by benches along each side. The table would accommodate probably eight men or thereabouts. One end of the room held a cast iron stove, where a gray-bearded cook held forth.

"Customer for you, Johnny. Fill him up, will you?"

Unlike the guard, Johnny looked friendly enough. He smiled and motioned Longarm toward the table. "Set down, son. I have an antelope stew cooking here. Ought to be just about ready for a man to eat. I'll bring you a bowl and you can give me your opinion." He flashed a grin and added, "But keep in mind whatever you say, I'll be the one feeding you as long as you stay here."

Longarm laughed and said, "Oh, I learned a long time ago that it never pays to piss off the cook." He took a seat close to the stove.

The guard, he noticed, had disappeared, taking Long-arm's double-action Colt with him.

Johnny served him a bowl of aromatic stew rich in meat and potatoes, with globules of fat floating on the steaming surface. He brought coffee, a plate of cold biscuits, and a pot of jam as well.

"You do know how to feed a man," Longarm said. "This smells better'n my old mama's cooking."

"Dig in. There's more where that comes from."

The stew tasted every bit as good as it smelled. Longarm barely had time enough to finish his third bowl of the stuff before the guard was back. This time there was no sign of Longarm's revolver and gunbelt.

"You done, mister?"

Longarm nodded.

"Then come with me. You can meet the boss. If he likes you, you can have that work I told you about."

Longarm got up from the table, thanked the cook, and followed the guard across the courtyard to the tower. Which was, he noticed when they came close, built of quarried stone rather than adobe brick. Someone had put a hell of a lot of work into this latter-day castle.

"In here."

He followed the guard into a large room where a bearded gentleman in a handsome suit was talking with a tall man, thin as a rawhide whip and looking just as tough as one, both men standing beside a cavernous fireplace, which at the moment was cold.

"Over here," the guard said, motioning Longarm to a settee or sofa that was covered with a spotted cowhide cured with the hair still on. A pair of large chairs matched the sofa, all three brown and white.

Longarm took the indicated seat and waited for the master of the manor to acknowledge his presence.

Lyon—the gentleman almost surely would be Henry Lyon—started toward Longarm, but the thin, deadly looking man stopped him with a touch on the elbow.

Longarm was staring at the thin fellow, thinking he should know that one. From a wanted poster perhaps. Or had he seen this man somewhere before? If so, he could not place him.

The thin man leaned over and whispered something to

Lyon. Whatever was said caused Lyon to stiffen, then whisper something in response.

Lyon abruptly left the room, taking a staircase to an upper floor, while the thin man smiled and sauntered across to stand in front of Longarm.

"Welcome to Camelot, Deputy," he said, a six-gun sliding into his hand. The smile he gave Longarm was one of triumph, definitely not of welcome. "Long, isn't it? Deputy U.S. marshal?"

"Well shit," Longarm said aloud.

So much for the idea of passing himself off as a drifting stranger.

"On your feet, Deputy." In a louder voice he said, "Jake. Come inside here. I have one for you but put him in the pit first. I think the boss is gonna want to get some information from him before he goes down below."

The guard, presumably named Jake, reappeared in the doorway. This time he also had a revolver in his hand.

"Shit," Longarm repeated, raising his hands and meekly surrendering to the inevitable.

Chapter 37

What they called the pit was just that. A long, fairly deep pit dug into the dense earth on the top of the mesa where Camelot had been built. There were four iron grates laid across the top of the pit. Longarm was mildly curious why there would be four. That was until the second grate from the end was lifted and he was flung bodily into the pit beneath it. Then he discovered that the one long pit was divided into four sections, each section separated from the others by sets of steel bars.

Longarm recognized the bars as being the kind sold to towns to construct prefabricated jail cells. Longarm had seen plenty of those in his time. Although not from the inside. All in all he would rather look at them from the other side. Obviously in this case Henry Lyon bought himself one jail cell and used those bars to make four underground cells.

Overhead the heavy iron grate clanged shut and Jake's footsteps receded.

Longarm stood, brushed himself off, and looked at his surroundings. There were no furnishings, not even a cot to lie on. There was a crumpled blanket tossed in one corner. He assumed that was to be his bed while he was confined in the pit. And there were two buckets. One held water, but no dipper or cup to drink from. The other . . . One sniff told him what that bucket was expected to be used for. At the moment it was, fortunately, empty.

He could see through the bars to the other cells. The pit to his left held a thin, bewhiskered figure who was either sleeping or passed out. The pit to his immediate right was empty. And at the far end he could see a small figure crouching in a corner, although the intervening bars made it impossible for him to get a good look at that person.

At least, he told himself, he got a good meal out of them before the bastards threw him in here.

He heard footsteps above and looked up to see the thin fellow standing over the pit. The man looked pleased with himself.

"You are one lucky son of a bitch," the man said. "I missed you that one time I got a shot off at you."

"You shot . . ." Longarm scowled. "That was you? Up in Wyoming?"

"I thought I got you. You dropped and I thought I hit you."

"You got the horse, not me."

The fellow grunted. "That explains it, doesn't it? Like I said. Lucky."

"Mind telling me who you are?" Longarm asked.

"So you can sic your dogs on me?" He laughed. "Not that I suppose it makes any difference. You won't be leaving here alive anyway. So sure, I'll give you my name. Even tell you my right name. It's Carlton Bannister."

"Bannister," Longarm repeated with a shake of his head. "I don't know the name. Can't recall ever seeing any flyers on you."

"Mostly I been called Bunny Adams," Bannister said. "What you might call my 'professional' name."

"Ah, now that name I know. Hell, Bunny, you're wanted in so many states I can't count that high. You're practically famous. Wanted for just about every crime on the books."

"Thank you, Long. I take that as a compliment."

"I didn't mean it as one."

"Oh, I understand that. Still and all . . ." Adams chuckled. "A man should be proud of his work, and I consider myself to be a craftsman. It hurts my feelings to see that you survived that time I shot at you. Now I'm just pleased to be able to correct that error. This time I'll know you are dead."

Bunny Adams—or Carlton Bannister—turned on his heel and went happily on his way.

Custis Long was not so pleased.

Still, this caged animal was not quite toothless. No one had bothered to search him after Jake took his Colt from him. Longarm still had the two shots in the derringer he carried in his vest pocket, and he had his folding pocket-knife as well.

Hell, he could take on Henry Lyon's private army with all that firepower, couldn't he?

Chapter 38

Toward evening two guards came past. They bypassed Long-arm's pit, however, and went to the last pit on the end. Together they lifted the grate up and one of them snarled, "All right, girl. Time for you to go see the man. Are you coming willingly this time?"

Longarm rose from where he had been sitting on the dirt floor and moved closer to the bars.

"To hell with you and to hell with him too," a female voice responded.

"Suit yourself." In a louder voice the guard said, "Boys!" and two more men came, these carrying a ladder.

All four of the guards now present climbed down into the pit, picked the girl up, and bodily carried her up the ladder and away, leaving the confining grate laid back.

There still was no movement from the man to Long-arm's left, and he was beginning to wonder if the fellow was alive. That question was answered when the man moaned and rolled onto his belly.

In that position Longarm could see that the man's back was horribly lacerated. His flesh had been sliced in long cuts, each oozing blood and pus. The poor son of a bitch had been whipped, likely with a teamster's blacksnake. Except that a teamster uses the crack of his whip to guide and encourage his team, never to touch or to harm them. This poor bastard had been flayed to the bone. Longarm could actually see pale cartilage or bone lying within some of the cuts.

He crossed to that side of the pit and knelt beside the bars.

"Mister. Can you hear me? Are you awake?"

His fellow prisoner groaned and his eyelids fluttered, then opened. He turned his head to look in Longarm's direction.

"Who . . . you?"

"Long," Longarm announced to the poor fellow. "Deputy U.S. marshal." He laughed, perhaps a little bitterly. "Here to make an arrest, you understand. Who are you that you're in such a state?"

"Name is Sam. S . . . S . . . Sam Childers." He took a deep breath. "Tried to get . . . away."

"From this pit?"

Childers shook his head slightly. "Down . . . below."

"I don't understand," Longarm said.

"Mine. Gold mine. Lousy ore. Takes lots . . . rock . . . to make it pay. Lyon keeps . . . slaves. Works them to death if . . . if he has to . . . to make the mine pay." Childers grunted, a sound that might have been intended as a laugh. "Small payroll, you see. Uses his . . . guards. Bastards ever' one. You see . . . what they done to me."

"Can you shift over here closer to the bars between us?" Longarm asked.

"Can . . . try."

It took some time and a great deal of effort, effort that must have been terribly painful, but Childers did as Longarm asked. He wriggled close to the bars.

"That's good," Longarm said. He took his handkerchief from his pocket, wet it in his water bucket, and gently bathed the whip slashes that crisscrossed Sam Childers's back.

"That feels good," Childers said. "Real good."

"Who is the girl at the other end?" Longarm asked.

"Men he captures he keeps to work down below. He has . . . had a few women too. Keeps them for sex. Don't know how many he has in the house. More than one. I'm sure of that." Childers seemed to be feeling stronger now that he was receiving Longarm's help.

"That girl. Been here maybe two weeks. He bought her . . . from some place. She fights him. Two, three times a day the bastard will have her dragged inside. Couple of his men hold her down while he rapes her. She could live comfort . . . comfortable. If she'd give in to him. But she doesn't. I think he is trying to break her spirit, but she's a strong-willed little thing. She fights the guards every time."

"Who do you think will win?" Longarm asked.

"Oh, he will. If he can't break her, he'll kill her."

Longarm grunted. "Could be she'd consider that a victory for her side."

"Yeah. She's tough, all right. And stubborn."

"Do they take the whip to her too?"

"No, they don't. She's pretty. I think he doesn't want to spoil that. But if he gets tired of trying to break her, I'm betting he'll kill her."

"Not to change the subject or anything," Longarm said, "but is there a way out of here?"

"I've been here . . . shit, I don't know how long now. Long enough to think an awful lot. And to lay here looking up at those bars. The ones that cover the pit aren't bolted down or anything, just laid over the hole. The pit is about eight feet deep. I'm thinking if I get strong enough, I could jump up and grab hold of the bars over your hole while I kick the bars over top of my hole. You see what I'm getting at?"

"Yeah, I do. That might could work."

"So it could. But then what the hell would I do when I got out of the pit? There's walls all around. Solid. With guards on top of the wall and at the gate. I seen them."

"How long have you been here?" Longarm asked.

"This is . . . what? June, maybe?"

"September," Longarm told him.

"I drifted past . . . or tried to go past . . . in November last year. So I been here ten months. Other guys have come by since then and been caught. Some of them died or been killed. They don't feed worth a shit, and if a man gets sick, they just let him die rather than take care of him." Childers grimaced and went stiff as a jolt of pain hit him. After he relaxed, he said, "You'll learn all this. They'll keep you here long enough to soften you up. Then you'll go down below. You'll likely swing a pick just like the rest of us."

"You keep saying 'down below,'" Longarm said. "What d'you mean by that?"

"At the bottom of this here mesa. We're . . . I don't know how deep inside it we are by now. Pretty long tunnel anyway."

"Adit," Longarm said.

"Huh?"

He smiled. "A hole in the ground is only a tunnel if it goes all the way through. If you haven't broke out the other end yet, it's called an adit."

"I didn't know that," Childers said.

"Yeah, it's interesting the shit you learn if you live in Colorado for a while. Lot's of mining hereabouts."

"Listen, could I ask you for a favor?" Childers asked.

"Sure."

"My back. It feels like it's on fire. Could you put some more of that cool water on it, please? That really feels good."

"Glad to," Longarm said, reaching for the water bucket.

Chapter 39

"You bastards!" the girl's voice was weak but defiant as, sometime after dark, the guards dumped her back into her hole and clanged the grate down over it again.

Longarm waited until the men above were gone, then whispered, "Are you all right, miss?"

"Who are you?"

"At the moment I seem to be another prisoner, but not for the same reasons as you. As it happens, I'm a deputy U.S. marshal. I came here to look into something, and it seems I found more than I was prepared to handle. Are you all right?"

He could hear her derisive snort. "Just fine and dandy, mister. Tonight the bastard said if I don't start being nice to him, he'll just turn me over to the guards and maybe then to the slaves. I'll kill myself before I let that happen. I'm . . . I was a good girl until I wound up here."

"What happened?"

"I suppose it is a sorry tale but not an uncommon one. I fell in love with the wrong man. He betrayed me. That is what it comes down to."

"I'm sorry, miss."

"Don't be. Henry Lyon is the bastard who will have to pay for this. I just hope he remembers me when he burns in the fires of Hell. I hope he screams my name. Well, screw him and all his kith and kin." She paused for a moment. "Can I ask you something, mister?"

"Of course."

"What does the word 'kith' mean anyway?"

Longarm could not help but laugh. It seemed an odd question under these circumstances. But it did show that the girl was far from being broken by her captors if she could think of a silly thing like that. "I'm not sure," he admitted.

"I know it," Sam Childers piped up from his cell. "It means friends, relatives, folks that live around you or are close to you. Kin, they all have to be related to you somehow. Kith don't."

"Thank you," the girl said.

"Is there anything we can do for you?" Longarm asked.

"You can pray for me. Would you do that, please? Both of you?"

"I will," Longarm promised.

"Me too," Childers said. "Can I tell you something?" he added.

"Sure."

"I saw you when they brought you in. You are . . . you're awful pretty."

"Maybe I was once, but I'm soiled goods now. No man will have me after this." She sounded entirely matter-of-fact about that prediction. Remarkably, there was no bitterness in her voice at all.

"Once you leave here," Longarm said, "no one needs to know the things that went on here."

"I'll know," the girl said, her voice very low and sorrowful.

"You can think about that after the three of us get out of here," Longarm told her.

"Mister, you are dreaming."

"No, I'm not. Sam told me how to do it."

"I did?"

"Sure you did. You said you were going to try it as soon as you were strong enough. Well, I'm strong enough."

"Maybe, but what happens after you get out?" Childers asked.

Longarm chuckled. "Oh, I have an idea or two about that too. Do you think you can help if we can get out of these cells? Physically I mean. Are you up to it?"

"I'll help or I'll die trying," Sam swore.

"Me too," the girl put in. "I would rather die than to be that man's slave for the rest of my life."

"All right then," Longarm said. "Now, first things first. Let's get up out of this damn hole so's we can maybe accomplish somethin'. Sam, I want you to . . . Oh, shit. Wait."

He could see a growing thread of light above the grate and could hear the approach of some of Lyon's guards. Men carrying a lantern, obviously.

"Long," one of the men called as they came near. "Stand up. The boss wants to see you."

Quickly Longarm plucked his pocket watch—with the .41-caliber derringer attached to the watch chain—out of his vest. He thrust both it and his pocketknife through the bars and said, "Hide these, Sam. Lie on top of them and pretend you're still passed out. They are what's gonna get us outa here. When I get back."

"If you get back," Childers said.

"I'm coming back." Longarm chuckled. "Hey, have I ever lied to you before?"

Even under these circumstances Sam Childers laughed.

The covering grate was shoved back and a ladder thrust

down into the pit. Longarm could see at least four men standing above the hole, one of them holding a lantern.

"Are you coming up on your own, Long, or do we have to come down and get you?"

"There's no need for violence, boys. Let me freshen up a mite and I'll be right pleased to join you." He made sure his shirttail was tucked in, tugged his vest down, and scampered up the ladder to see what fate had in store for him this time.

Chapter 40

They took him to the same large room with the fireplace, except now there was a fire blazing on the hearth, cedar judging by the fragrance it gave off. The room was bright as day, in fact much brighter now than it had been in daytime, courtesy of a dozen lamps blazing along the walls. Bunny Adams was there, lean and lethal, as was Henry Lyon, who now was wearing a satin dressing gown.

This evening, Longarm noticed, Bunny had a coiled bullwhip draped over his shoulder. His left shoulder, where it would not interfere if he needed to get his six-gun out in a hurry.

Lyon took a seat in one of the armchairs, crossed his legs, and took a fat cigar from a small humidor that rested on a small table nearby. He struck a match, then slowly and very carefully warmed the cigar before clamping it between his teeth and lighting it. The smoke smelled good, although not as pleasant as the scent from the burning cedar.

The master of the manor—Longarm had already come to the realization that Senator Lyon was quite mad—motioned with one finger, and his thugs grasped Longarm by the upper arm and guided him to a spot directly in front of Lyon and about six feet away. Obviously they thought it a safe distance. In truth Longarm could kill Lyon, perhaps Bunny Adams too, before the guards could stop him. He felt sure that he could. A quick blow to the throat and a violent wrench of the neck and it would be done.

Of course then there would be the small problem of the four guards. They would not stand idly by and allow it to happen.

Longarm had no intention of offering himself as a sacrifice. His moment would come. But not now.

"Bring me a brandy," Lyon said, looking at Adams.

Longarm doubted that the man particularly wanted a brandy. What he did want was to demonstrate his control over Bunny Adams. He had the killer on a leash and wanted this deputy marshal to know it and be cowed by it.

Bunny dutifully went to the sideboard and poured his master the requested drink.

"I'll take one of those too, Bunny."

Adams merely scowled, but Lyon accepted the brandy and said, "Do pour one for him, Bunny. And one for yourself if you like." He smiled, although there was no trace of warmth or friendliness in the expression. "We do try to be hospitable here, Mr. Long."

"Very kind of you, I'm sure," Longarm said dryly.

Bunny poured another brandy and brought it to Longarm. He did not take one for himself.

"Thanks," Longarm said, raising the glass and inhaling the aroma of the brandy. Brandy was not his preferred tipple, but even he could tell that this was an exceptionally good one. He tasted it and found it to be smooth and pleasant on the tongue. "Very nice," he said.

"I am so glad you approve. Would you care to sit?"

"I'll stand, thanks."

"That is all right. What I have to say will not take long."

Longarm took another small sip of the brandy.

"There are things I would like you to tell me. If you do talk to me, openly and honestly, I will grant you your life. You will be allowed to work for me in my gold mine. That may be a difficult life for you, but you will be allowed to live."

"And the alternative?" Longarm asked.

"If you fail to answer my questions, Mr. Adams here will have the pleasure of using that whip of his. He is very good with it. He can hit the same spot. Over and over again. He can cut limbs off that way. I have seen him do it. Why, he can practically dismember a person before they have the relief of death to free them from the agony. Believe me, Marshal, you do not want to experience that. It will be much better for you to tell me what I want to know. And my questions are really very simple. Basically it boils down to what you have reported back to Marshal Vail . . . a very good man, by the way; I know him well from my work in the capital . . . and who else you may have told about my little . . . my fiefdom, you might call it." The mirthless smile flickered onto his face again. "That will be easy enough, will it not?"

Lyon took a sip of his brandy and said, "Well?"

"Well fuck you very much, but I think not," Longarm responded.

"I rather suspected you would feel that way, so Bunny will give you a small foretaste of what you can expect. Then tomorrow morning you will be asked again. If you still refuse to cooperate with me, I will have you taken down below so all my slaves can witness your pain. Your pain will serve as an example to them, you see. It is good for a slave to understand the price of disobedience, so you will serve me whether you wish to or not.

"I will have you tied in place, and Bunny here will use his blacksnake to very slowly cut you apart, one small piece at a time while the slaves all watch. And listen.

"But it needn't come to that, Long. You can choose to preserve your life by simply telling me all I want to know. That will undoubtedly anger Bunny, but it will save your life. Think about it tonight, Long. I shall ask you again tomorrow." He nodded toward Adams.

While Longarm's attention was on the madman Lyon, Bunny had taken the blacksnake from his shoulder and shaken it out. Now he took a step forward and suddenly lashed out with the whip.

The rawhide popper found its mark just above Longarm's left knee. It cut through his corduroy trousers as cleanly as a knife. And almost as deep. Longarm felt like a hot branding iron had just been laid across his flesh.

"Jeez!" he cried out. He tried to back away from the whip, only to discover the guards' hands clamped like iron on his upper arms, keeping him in place where he was.

The whip snaked out again, but this time the tip cut only cloth, leaving the skin beneath that cloth untouched.

"You see, Long, I can cut wherever I wish, and it will be my pleasure tomorrow to show you just how much pain a man can stand," Adams said. He sounded eager for the chance to kill with that long and deadly bullwhip.

"Go to hell, Adams."

"In due time perhaps, but not until you're dead, Long."

"That is enough, Bunny," Lyon put in. "You made your point. Long, think about what I have told you. We will speak again in the morning. You have until then to make up your mind." With a curt nod to his guards, he sent Longarm staggering out of the room, his left leg still afire and his arms secured by the guards.

That whip was awfully damned persuasive; the son of a bitch *hurt*!

Chapter 41

There was no ladder this time. The guards merely walked him to the rim of the pit and gave him a shove. Longarm fell the eight or nine feet to the bottom of the pit and landed with a thump. The air rushed out of him, and he was left writhing in pain and gasping for breath while the heavy iron grate was again laid over his underground cell.

"Bastards," he snarled when he again had breath enough to speak, but by then the guards—and their lantern—had returned to whatever hole they crawled into.

"Are you all right, Long?" Sam Childers asked from the other side of the bars.

"No. That son of a bitch Adams tagged me one with his fuckin' bullwhip."

"Just once?"

"Yeah, but that was enough. Teachin' me a lesson, they said."

"Believe it," Childers said. "I saw him kill a man with that whip once. Killed him slow and deliberate. Poor son of a bitch died hard, I can tell you, and the worst of it was that

Adams enjoyed it. You could see it on his face. He liked killing that way. Liked it. Jesus!"

"That man is evil," the girl put in from her end of the dark pit. "He gives me the creeps. I don't think Henry Lyon knows it, but when Henry is done with me and they are bringing me back here, Adams likes to feel me up. He touches me, and when I try to pull away, he laughs. He likes for people to be afraid of him, and I think he likes it that he disgusts everyone. I think I hate him even more than I hate Henry."

"With any kinda luck, missy, we won't none of us have to worry about Bunny Adams or Henry Lyon either one. We're fixing to get outa here."

"Do you really think so?" the girl asked.

"Yeah, kid, I do."

"I'm scared."

"Good. You should be. Sam, d'you think you're strong enough to get outa here if I can get these grates pushed off of us?"

"I'll make it," Childers said, determination steeling his voice. "If you can do that, Long, I'll do my part."

"Good. Give me back my derringer then. You keep the knife. Girl. Are you up to this?"

"Just give me a chance. I'm ready."

Longarm stood. He put his back against the bars that separated him from Childers's cell and jumped up to grab hold of the grate that covered his part of the pit.

He hung there for a moment, then shifted his hands through the bars so that he was holding onto the grate above Sam's cell, leaving the grate over his own free of his weight.

Longarm jackknifed his body, planted his feet onto the grate, and pushed. The heavy grate barely moved.

He tried again. Pushed harder. There was a little more movement this time.

"Son of a bitch!" he said as, his arms tiring, he dropped away from the grate and once again hung straight down.

Longarm dropped down and landed on the floor.

"You can't do it?" Childers asked. "Is it hopeless?"

"Hell, no, it ain't hopeless, Sam. I told you we're gonna get outa here, and we will. Just give me a minute to rest my arms. We'll do it. If not this next time, then the time after that. Or the time after that one. However long it takes, we'll get it done."

"Can I help?" the girl asked.

"Yeah. Pray," Longarm said.

"I've been doing that, Marshal."

"Good. Keep it up." Longarm swung his arms around a bit to loosen his muscles, then repeated his movements: jumped up to hang from the grate, moved his hands to cling to Sam's grate instead of his own, swung his boots up to contact the iron grate above his cell, and . . . pushed.

He gave the grate all the power he could muster.

It moved. Not more than six inches perhaps, but it was pushed aside.

Longarm was smiling when he pushed again. And again after that. In a few minutes he had his cell partially uncovered. Enough for him to fit through.

Then it was only a matter of climbing the steel bars between his cell and Sam's until he stood free in the cool night air with nothing but a few distant stars above him.

Chapter 42

Sam Childers was weak. He managed to climb halfway up the cell bars. Longarm helped him the rest of the way from there. There was enough pale light from the stars for Longarm to see the broad grin on Childers's face.

"Free," he said.

"Yeah. But keep your voice down," Longarm cautioned. "Come on now. Help me get the girl out."

With both of them pulling, they were able to get the grate over that pit out of the way in no time at all, then both men leaned down at the edge of her pit.

"Jump," Longarm whispered. "Reach high as you can and jump. Me and Sam will grab your wrists and pull you up."

"All right. Here I come."

Longarm missed his first attempt to reach her. Childers caught her left wrist but was not strong enough to hold her. He let go and she fell back into the pit.

"Are you all right?" Sam asked.

"I'm fine."

"Jump again," Longarm said. "Quick now. We don't want

to be out here in the middle of this damn courtyard any longer than we got to."

The girl jumped, and this time Longarm caught her wrist. Sam missed his hold on her, but she weighed little and Longarm was able to lift her out of the pit by himself.

"Look, uh, I don't know if you've noticed this, young lady, but you ain't wearing any clothes," Longarm said.

"You know, I did notice that," she returned, "but thank you for mentioning it."

As a matter of fact she had a lovely body. Which Longarm could not help noticing. She was slim, with long, blond hair, delicate features, and firm, perky breasts. He could understand why any man would want her. But to hold on her terms, not as chattel.

"Are you all right?" he asked, pulling off his tweed coat and giving it to her.

"Better now that I'm out of that hellhole," she said. She put Longarm's coat on. It did not cover her completely, but it was better than nothing. She rolled the sleeves up and bobbed her head. "I'm ready."

"Come on," Longarm said. "Let's get outa this place."

With Longarm leading the way, the three headed for the tunnel that led to the outside world and to freedom.

Chapter 43

"Wait here," Longarm whispered.

A pale yellow beam of light spread for several yards into the courtyard, coming from an open doorway beside the entry. That would be where the guards had come out behind him when he first arrived at Senator Lyon's damned castle. Senator Lyon's castle of the damned would be more appropriate, Longarm thought.

Derringer in hand, he peered around the doorjamb. A single guard sat at a table with a newspaper spread out before him and a lamp burning nearby. His lips were moving as he sounded out the words.

The man was imposingly large but probably not very bright. Perfect material for this kind of work. He would do what he was told, whatever that happened to be, and if it caused pain to some other human being, well, that was not his problem, was it?

It was for this fellow and others like him that Lyon intended to make the girl a plaything if she did not agree to serve as his slave. In Longarm's opinion it would be criminal—criminal both morally and in law—for her delicate beauty and spunk to be broken on the shoals of thugs like this son of a bitch.

He was already pissed off at the unsuspecting guard when he silently slipped into the small guard room.

A rack containing two repeating rifles and a sawed-off shotgun sat beside the adobe outer wall, and the guard was wearing a revolver on his belt. Longarm saw his own gunbelt lying on a low side table. With that much armament he figured he could take on Henry Lyon's entire damned army.

Which was a good thing because he very likely would have to do exactly that.

"What the fuck?" the huge guard mumbled at Longarm's approach.

"Time to pay the piper, asshole," Longarm snarled.

He thrust the derringer hard against the center of the guard's chest. "Stay where you are an' don't move," he ordered. "You got some handcuffs or heavy manacles around here, I'm sure o' that. Where are they?"

"Little man, you just fucked up. Now I am gonna break you in two." The guard stood. He towered over Longarm, and Longarm was well over six feet tall himself. This guard was huge.

Ignoring the revolver at his belt, the fellow reached for Longarm's throat.

Longarm had no intention of letting that ape get his hands on him. He pulled the trigger of the derringer, and a .41-caliber slug along with a spray of fiery gases burst inside the man's chest, shattering his heart and dropping him instantly to the floor. The walls of his chest cavity contained both the sound and the fury of the gunshot, so there was only a muffled pop to be heard. Longarm doubted the sound traveled any farther than the doorway.

Very quickly he retrieved his gunbelt and took a moment

to check his Colt to make sure no one had tampered with it and that it was still fully loaded.

"Psst! You can come in now," he whispered to Sam Childers and the girl.

"Here." He took one of the lever-action rifles—Marlins, good guns, he noticed—and tossed it to Sam. The other he took for himself. He stripped the gunbelt off the dead guard and gave that to Sam too.

"I can take that shotgun," the girl said. "My grampa taught me how to hunt game since I was knee-high."

"All right, but this game walks on their hind legs. Think you can do it?"

The girl ignored the question and stalked to the back of the room. She picked up the shotgun and stuffed a handful of shells into the pocket of Longarm's tweed coat.

Damned coat looked an awful lot better on her than it ever had on him, Longarm conceded.

He grabbed a box of .44-40s off a shelf for himself and another for Sam, then checked to make sure his rifle was fully loaded. It was.

"I want you two to slip out of this miserable excuse for a place," he said. "Head for Craig. There's a road of sorts that'll take you right to it. When you get there, tell the county sheriff what's been going on here. Have him send a posse back this way to pick up some prisoners."

"Where will you be while we're off fetching the sheriff?" Sam asked.

"Me, I got business here with Bunny Adams and with the Right Honorable Senator Lyon." He smiled, but the expression held no warmth. "And with any of their pals that want to take a hand in this."

"Go ahead then," Childers said. "I'm right behind you." He turned to the girl and added, "You go outside and hide. Me and Long will be along directly."

"Like hell you say," the girl retorted. "Don't you even think about sending me off by myself like that." She hefted the shotgun and grinned. "I'm scared of the dark."

Damn but Longarm did like this girl's spirit. Henry Lyon had not even come close to breaking her. And never would, Longarm guessed. The man could kill her but would never break her.

"Well I'm not gonna stand here all night arguin' with the two of you, so follow along and stay outa the way."

He stuffed his pants pockets with .44-40s and extinguished the lamp so he could take a few moments for his eyes to adjust to the darkness. Then, Childers and girl on his heels, he headed out into the night.

Chapter 44

The interior of the castle keep—or whatever the hell they called the tall building—was lighted bright as day. Sounds of merriment suggested someone in there was celebrating. Or possibly this was just an average, everyday night for these merry men. Longarm neither knew nor cared. What he did know was that the sound of their partying was more than loud enough to cover any noises he and his "troops" might make.

He stepped inside, then turned to glance back at the two on his heels. It was impossible to avoid noticing how very attractive the girl was wearing his coat, all blond hair at one end and shapely legs at the other. No wonder Lyon was so infatuated with her.

Placing a finger over his lips to advise silence, he crept toward the main hall and the revelers.

Longarm stood in the doorway. There were—he counted—seven men gathered with drinks in their hands, surrounding two young, very pretty—and very naked— women on the floor in the middle of the room. The girls were engaged in the position commonly known as a sixty-nine. When one of them lifted her head away from contact with the pussy of her companion, the men cursed and lashed her with belts.

This, then, was the sort of fate the girl behind him would have had if she were turned over to Lyon's men. Probably these girls had belonged to Lyon to begin with but were relegated to pleasing the guards once the senator tired of them.

The more he learned about this crowd, the more Longarm was pissed off by them. Bringing these bastards down was going to be a very great pleasure, he thought.

Longarm stepped inside.

There were more of them than there were of him. And anyway he saw no reason to give mercy to animals like these. Gunsmoke and lead were what they deserved.

And what they got.

One of the seven saw Longarm and his two companions standing there. The fellow moved his hand. It was remotely possible that he was raising his hands in surrender, more likely that he was going for the revolver on his hip.

Longarm neither knew nor cared which. He drew back the hammer of his Marlin and sent his first carefully aimed shot into the face of a burly redhead who seemed to be having fun beating the helpless girls.

The fellow's head snapped back and a red mist hung in the air as a good portion of his brains flew in the direction of the fireplace.

Longarm continued firing, cranking out bullets as rapidly as he could lever a fresh cartridge into the chamber and trip the trigger again.

He was aware without really looking that Sam had moved up beside him and was also shooting.

Not a one of the guards so much as got a gun in hand. They all died in a wild tangle of bodies and blood.

The room filled quickly with pale smoke, the normally

pleasant smell of burned gunpowder so heavy it coated the insides of his nostrils and stank, the smell of it mingling with the lighter copper scent of spilled blood.

The shooting was over in a matter of seconds. The two girls froze in place.

Longarm walked over to them and nudged one in the butt with the muzzle of his rifle.

"Ouch, dammit, that thing is hot, mister," she protested.

"Sorry. Tell you what, little missy, whyn't you and your friend here grab some clothes an' scamper the hell outa here. There's hell to pay for Henry Lyon and his friends this night, and you're better off out of it."

"You don't have to tell me twice, mister." The girl grabbed the hand of her partner and broke for the outside.

"Now what?" Sam Childers asked.

Longarm's ears were still ringing from the concussive pounding of so many gunshots inside a closed space, but he managed to hear what Sam was asking.

"Now we go hunting," Longarm told him. "Neither Lyon nor Bunny Adams is in this pile o' cooling meat," he said, gesturing toward the pile of dead at his feet. "I don't figure to let them get away, and now they will have got warned by all the shooting." He grinned. "It just gets harder from here on, but it's something I best handle on my own. Two of us would just get in each other's way in close quarters. What I want you to do, Sam, is to cover my backside. I want you at the outside door. I want you to keep any other guards, if there be any, from comin' in behind me. Can you do that?"

"Damn right I can," Childers said, busily stuffing fresh cartridges into his rifle.

"Good man. I'm counting on you." Longarm reloaded his own rifle and headed for the staircase that led up to Lyon's private quarters.

Chapter 45

Sam Childers raced ahead of Longarm, shouldering past him before Longarm reached the stone staircase and then taking the steps two at a time, his rifle held at the ready.

It was Sam's right to confront Lyon, Longarm conceded. After all, he had suffered much more abuse at the senator's hands than Longarm ever had, so Longarm followed several paces behind.

Sam's head barely came higher than the second-floor landing when he stopped, eyes widening as he tried to swing his rifle sideways toward something on that floor that Longarm could not yet see.

It was too late.

Longarm heard a sudden flurry of gunshots, and the back of Sam's head exploded as one bullet after another punched into him.

The man died instantly, his body crumpling onto the stairs and rolling down into Longarm's legs.

Without taking time for conscious thought, Longarm reached down. He grabbed Sam's lifeless body by the shoulder and heaved the bloody thing aside, tossing it off the stairs and out of the way. It was a callous way to treat what so recently was a living being, but Longarm was busy at the moment.

Busy trying to remember the exact sequence of the shots he'd heard fired. Trying to remember how many there had been.

Four? Five? He thought perhaps five.

If so—and if they had come from a revolver rather than a rifle—whoever was up there was empty or close to it. The shooter more than likely was now intent on reloading.

With the ringing from all the shooting down below still blocking his ears, Longarm could not hear well enough to tell if brass was hitting the floor, as would be the case if someone up there was punching out his empties.

He hesitated just a heartbeat or two, just long enough, he hoped, for the shooter to think there was no one on Sam Childers's heels. Just long enough to give the shooter the idea that he had time enough to reload.

Then Longarm set his rifle down on the stairs and palmed his Colt, the shorter arm being easier to swing to the side, that being where the shots had come from that hammered poor Sam Childers.

With his .45 at the ready, Longarm bounded the last few steps up to the landing.

His weathered face split into a joyous grin when he cleared the floor and could see into the second-story room.

Bunny Adams was there. The gunsel was intent on re-loading a single-action Remington revolver. Longarm caught him with the gun in his left hand while his right was working the extractor pin.

Bunny cursed and threw the Remington at Longarm's head, clearly hoping to make Longarm duck and perhaps lose his footing on the stone steps.

It did not work.

Longarm laughed and triumphantly declared, "Adams, or Bannister, or whatever the hell your name is today, I am placing you under arrest for the murder of Sam Childers and God knows how many more souls."

Adams straightened to his full height and squared his shoulders. "Bastard," he hissed.

"Tell me something, Bunny. Was that you that shot Moses Arthur up there in Cheyenne?"

Adams grunted. "That was me. The senator couldn't have some stupid old son of a bitch like that messing things up for him, now could he? The senator is going to form his own independent nation here, you see. He has it all worked out. But where the Confederacy went wrong was in trying to completely secede. The senator's nation will be a . . . he called it a protectorate of the United States. Like an Indian tribe, see, but for white men only. Like I say, he has it all worked out and I'll be his number two in command. I'll have my own slaves and everything. And I am *not* going to allow the likes of you to ruin his dream."

With that Bunny reached behind him.

Longarm was not at all surprised that the man would have a backup gun.

Longarm's Colt roared, his first shot striking Bunny just above the belt buckle, the second in the chest as the recoil from a squat .45 cartridge lifted the muzzle, and his third shot taking Bunny in the throat.

Bunny Adams, real name Carlton Bannister, was very likely dead before his body hit the floor.

Chapter 46

Longarm walked to the set of wooden stairs that led up to the third floor. "Henry. Are you up there, Henry? I'm coming for you, Senator. You are under arrest, Senator. Or maybe you're dead. That'd be your choice." While he spoke, taunting the delusional state senator, he was busy reloading his Colt. The three remaining in the cylinder would probably be enough, but "probably" was not nearly good enough. He intended to have a full cylinder when he confronted the man.

Revolver recharged, Longarm took the stairs. But slowly. He did not want to be caught exposed the way Sam Childers had been.

The greatest danger would be when his head reached the level of the floor above. Not knowing exactly where his enemy was would put him at a disadvantage, and in a gunfight there was no such thing as fair play. There were only a victor and a vanquished. Custis Long damn sure intended to be the victor.

"Did you hear me, Henry? You're under arrest."

If Lyon would just respond—in any way at all—hurl insults, move around on the wooden floor, any damn thing— it might give Longarm a clue as to where he was.

There was . . . nothing.

Longarm stopped on the steps and listened, his hearing beginning to return but doing him no good until or unless Lyon did something to give himself away.

He heard nothing at all from that floor. Nothing.

Well, if Lyon was not going to move, Longarm would have to.

He very slowly went up one more step. And another.

The top of his head came level with the floorboards. He poked it quickly up and back down again. He did not know where his Stetson was or he would have teased Lyon with a peek at that first.

There was just nothing else to do, he realized, but to hold his Colt high and ready and take that last step to fully expose his head.

He took a deep breath and willed his pounding heart to slow. Then he stepped up to find . . . nothing.

The room on that floor was empty save for a bed, a wardrobe—some poor sons of bitches must have had themselves a time getting that big old thing up these narrow stairs—a chest, and a dressing table.

There was no sign of Henry Lyon.

A final set of stairs, however, more like a ladder than a staircase, led to the tower above.

Lyon pretty much had to be there.

Once again Custis Long faced the daunting test of exposing himself to an enemy while he climbed up to make an arrest.

It was something that had to be done, however, so Longarm, grimacing and growling, did it.

He reached the summit of Henry Lyon's castle without incident.

The senator—and would-be dictator of his own slave-holding nation—was there, standing beneath the banner emblazoned with a lion in honor of . . . himself.

Lyon did not look very much in charge of anything right now. Not even himself. He was trembling and in a dressing gown again. He appeared to be unarmed.

Longarm stepped off the stairs to the more secure footing of the tower platform.

"You're under arrest, Lyon. For lots of shit. We'll work out the exact charges later."

Lyon lifted his chin defiantly. "You have no cause to arrest me, Long. Murder is not a federal crime. You have no jurisdiction here anyway, as this is an independent protectorate of your United States of America. I make the laws here. Not you or yours."

"All right, Mr., uh, how should I address you? As 'Your Majesty,' perhaps?"

"Your Excellency will do," Lyon said. He seemed entirely serious about it too. He was not trying to make a joke, never mind that he was in fact doing so without realizing it. And that seemed rather sad. The stupid son of a bitch was somewhere out of his mind.

"How about I just call you 'under arrest,' Henry? If you think about it, you might could remember that slavery is outlawed by the Constitution, and that's what I'm arresting you for. Like I said, we'll work out the entire list of charges when I've got you safely behind bars."

"I intend to lodge a protest about this, young man."

"You do that, Henry. In the meantime put your hands behind your back."

Lyon stood quietly, still defiant but not moving. Not reaching for any sort of weapon.

Longarm became aware that the girl had followed him up the stairs. Now she emerged onto the tower floor. She was still carrying the sawed-off shotgun she had taken from the guard room, although she had not fired the 12-gauge in the gunfight below.

She stared at the man who had kidnapped and repeatedly raped her.

Lyon looked at the nearly naked girl and sneered. "You look lovely, dear. How about giving me one last piece of ass before you are sent off to a brothel somewhere."

The girl stepped around Longarm to directly confront Senator Henry Leon Lyon.

With deliberate care she pulled back the hammers of the shotgun and fired, the flame from her left barrel lighting up the pale predawn, the heavy charge of lead buckshot hitting Lyon in the crotch. Her right barrel wiped his face off his skull.

Then she dropped the shotgun and burst into tears.

She would not be crying for Henry Lyon, Longarm was sure, and neither would he.

"You can arrest me now," she said.

"Why?" he asked. "You heard what the man said. I'm a federal officer an' murder ain't a federal crime. I got no jurisdiction to arrest you, little miss. Now, let's us go down and see if there's any more shooting to do."

Chapter 47

If there were any guards, they had time to scamper. And they did. Longarm could find no sign of them, although the friendly cook was in his kitchen. The man did not seem particularly distressed to learn that his boss and the guards were dead.

"It was time I move along anyway," he said.

"Where are the slaves kept?" Longarm asked.

"C'mon. I'll show you."

The girls, three very pretty young women, were locked inside a small room off the castle courtyard. They came out squawking like a flock of geese and ran for a path leading down off the mesa.

The girl who shot Lyon had discarded her shotgun. Now she went inside the slave quarters long enough to retrieve a dress and a bonnet. She returned Longarm's tweed coat. Longarm thought she looked even prettier once she had her dignity back.

"Where will you be going now?" she asked.

"Down to free the slaves outa Lyon's mine. Then I need

to find some horses so's I can get you someplace civilized. Could I ask you somethin', miss?"

"I owe you my life, Marshal. You can ask me anything."

"What's your name? It seems strange, but in all this time and through all that's happened, I don't have no notion of who you are."

"My name is Justine, Marshal. Justine Crowne."

"Good Lord. You're the reason I came here. Your grampa Arthur died tryin' to tell me about you."

"Gramp Mose is dead too? And my grampa and gramma Crowne are gone. So is their place. I don't know where my daddy is. I'm all alone now."

Longarm smiled. "No, you ain't, Justine, and soon as we find us some horses I am gonna take you to your mama. She's been fretting about you, y'know."

Justine squealed with pleasure and hugged him.

Longarm swallowed. Hard. Justine was one damned pretty girl, and they were about to set off on a very long trip back to Medicine Bow.

It just might, he thought, turn out to be a very *interesting* trip as well as a long one.

Watch for

LONGARM AND THE DOOMED BEAUTY

The 397th novel in the exciting LONGARM
series from Jove

Coming in December!

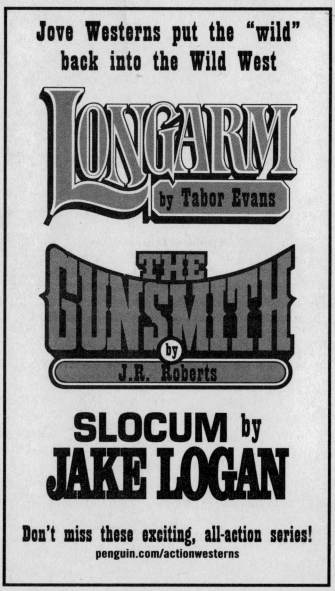